Dear Reader,

As a child, I a... ...rliest memories is ... ...d hardcover of Hans Christian Andersen's collection. I loved the magic and atmosphere, the sense of right and wrong, good versus bad, the moralism and hope, and I always, always wished for a happy ending. My love for these fairy tales turned me into a bonafide romance reader. After all, the best romance novels have so much in common with the most enduring fairy tales.

Combining two of my favorite stories into this mash-up was such fun. I wanted to bring Cinderella into the twenty-first century, and Lucinda is just the perfect modern-day heroine. Unfortunately for Lucinda, the path to achieving her goals lies with Thirio: the beast. A long-ago trauma leaves him determined to be miserable and alone. Only Lucinda's determination to succeed conflicts with Thirio's life of solitude... Can he live with the consequences?

The last couple of years have taken their toll on all of us! We need happy endings more than ever. I hope you adore Thirio and Lucinda every bit as much as I do.

Thanks for reading,

Clare x

Clare Connelly was raised in small-town Australia among a family of avid readers. She spent much of her childhood up a tree, Harlequin book in hand. Clare is married to her own real-life hero, and they live in a bungalow near the sea with their two children. She is frequently found staring into space—a surefire sign she is in the world of her characters. She has a penchant for French food and ice-cold champagne, and Harlequin novels continue to be her favorite-ever books. Writing for Harlequin Presents is a long-held dream. Clare can be contacted via clareconnelly.com or on her Facebook page.

Books by Clare Connelly

Harlequin Presents

My Forbidden Royal Fling
Crowned for His Desert Twins

Signed, Sealed...Seduced

Cinderella's Night in Venice

The Cinderella Sisters

Vows on the Virgin's Terms
Forbidden Nights in Barcelona

Clare Connelly

CINDERELLA IN THE BILLIONAIRE'S CASTLE

ISBN-13: 978-1-335-58358-1

Cinderella in the Billionaire's Castle

Copyright © 2022 by Clare Connelly

Recycling programs
for this product may
not exist in your area.

Harlequin Enterprises ULC
22 Adelaide St. West, 41st Floor
Toronto, Ontario M5H 4E3, Canada
www.Harlequin.com

Printed in U.S.A.

CINDERELLA IN THE
BILLIONAIRE'S CASTLE

PROLOGUE

Six years earlier

'YOU AREN'T SERIOUSLY going out, Thirio?'

With his dark eyes rimmed with mirth and his almost too handsome face cocked at a curious angle, Thirio grinned. It was a grin that was known all over the world, certainly all over the tabloids and gossip blogs. 'Why wouldn't I?'

Constantina's lips pursed with obvious disapproval. And behind the disapproval, there was something more. Concern. She took a step into her son's palatial bedroom. 'Well, for one thing, tomorrow is your father's birthday. Hundreds of people are coming to spend the day, and he's going to expect—' She furrowed her brow. '*We* are going to expect you to be a part of the celebrations.'

'I'm not planning to miss it, Mother. Relax.'

Constantina moved deeper into his room, regarding her handsome boy—a man, now, really—through narrowed green eyes. 'Must you go out every night?'

Thirio turned, a petulant curl to his wide-set mouth. 'Does it really matter?'

'You're wasting your life.'

'What else would you have me do? Lie by the pool all day? Go and play golf? Sail about the Med in a yacht?'

'You could come to work with us,' Constantina pointed out, the position that had been created for him at Skartos Inc. one that had sat vacant since Thirio's eighteenth birthday. Thirio Skartos, born into one of the oldest, wealthiest families in Europe, did not *need* to work. The trust fund he'd been granted access to was filled with billions of pounds, and he intended to spend his way through each and every one of them. Hedonism felt good.

'I'm here, Mother. I came back for his party. Don't push it.'

Constantina sighed heavily. There was so much of her husband in their son. When she looked at Thirio's face, she could see Andreas. All his strength, pride and stubborn determination. She stood slowly, the sadness impossible to conceal from her delicate features. She didn't meet Thirio's gaze, so didn't see the answering hint of remorse that briefly creased the corners of his lips.

'I didn't come here to fight.'

'We're not fighting.' Remorse washed away, leaving a brilliant smile in its place.

'But, Thirio, you are off course. How can you

live your life like this? Women, alcohol, parties. This is not how we raised you!'

'Isn't it?'

Constantina flinched, the accusation landing right in the centre of her heart. She thought of all the nights she and Andreas had gone out, or entertained, of the children they'd allowed to be raised by a mix of boarding schools, nannies and, in the holidays, a doting *yiayia*.

'You could be so much more.'

'How I live my life is none of your concern.'

Constantina pursed her lips. 'You are wrong, darling. And I *am* concerned.' She moved towards the door, innate elegance in every step. 'Please, do not infect your sister with this attitude. She is seventeen years old and thank God seems to want more from her life than the perennially low expectations you have set for yourself.'

'Heaven forbid Queen Evie should let her hair down a little,' he said with a heavenward roll of his eyes. 'If you ask me, she could do with a bit more fun—'

'Well, I'm not asking you,' Constantina denounced. 'Do not lead her astray, Thirio.'

'I'm here for Dad's party. I will talk to the guests, smile for the photos, and then leave. Happy?'

Constantina was far from happy. She had always adored Thirio. He had been the kind of little boy it had been impossible not to love: chubby and sweet with a ready smile and a delightfully bossy nature, even as a toddler. But at some point, he'd changed. Oh, he was still doted on. Feted, even. His good looks and natural intelligence made him popular socially, but his Midas touch had also made him arrogant and self-assured to a fault.

He will grow out of it, Andreas always insisted, with enough of a smile for Constantina to understand that her husband looked on their son's misdeeds with a far kinder eye.

'You are my child and I love you, Thirio. I always will. But there are times when I wish I could give you a healthy dose of reality. Can you not see what a gilded, privileged life you lead? Do you not wish to make something of yourself?' She shook her head sadly. 'You have all the opportunities in the heavens. You are smarter than anyone I know. You could change the world if only you would put your mind to it.'

Thirio's eyes narrowed. 'It's my life and I'll live it however I want.'

A spark of anger ignited in Constantina's belly. Thirio's wasted potential was a constant source of pain for the loving mother. 'Then let us both hope you start to live it better soon.'

She stalked from the room before she could say anything worse—though neither of them could have known those were the very last words she would ever speak to her son. Neither of them could have known that Constantina would not get the chance to see her son's life play out, her death, in the end, a tragedy of Thirio's making—a curse of sorts, that would haunt him for a great many years to come.

CHAPTER ONE

ON THE FEW occasions each year when Thirio absolutely had to leave the Castile di Neve, he always returned a foul-tempered beast. There was very little of the outside world that pleased him, and being forced to take part in it was an exercise that weighed heavily on his shoulders. Until finally he could fly his helicopter from whichever city he'd been obliged to visit, leaving civilisation behind, flying over the alpine forests for which these mountainous ridges were famed, drawing closer and closer to the castle he had, for the last six years, called home.

It rose from the cliff faces like a spectre of magic. On cloudy afternoons, the turrets of the towers appeared almost to hover, free-floating miles above the ravines that fell all the way to northern Italy, and, despite the romantic beauty of the centuries-old towers, Thirio felt an affinity with the ruggedness of their positioning.

They too did not belong.

And so here they stayed, two outcasts on the

edges of civilisation. It was almost impossible to remember now the parties his parents used to throw here, the way the castle used to hum with life and joy.

As Thirio brought his helicopter lower, circling around the castle to the landing pad at the rear, he saw something that made him swallow a dark curse.

A car.

Small and black, parked right near the front door to the *castile*.

One of the things Thirio liked most about the castle was how inaccessible it was. Sure, there was a road, but it was narrow and winding and, with the *castile* the natural end point of the road, tourist traffic never went past. Out here, he was completely alone. Which was how he damn well wanted it.

He'd woken in a foul mood—the prospect of needing to travel always did that—and his mood had only worsened as the day went on. All he'd wanted was to get home and shower, to wash away the memories of other people, of his past, his history, his guilt.

He cut the rotor blades but stayed in the helicopter as they slowed, trying to bring his temper under control. He expelled a long, slow breath, his nostrils flaring, then pushed open the side door. It was crisp up here, despite the fact that spring was reaching through the rest of the northern hemisphere, bringing flowers, sunshine and optimism. At the top of the world, the clouds were grey, the trees heavy with fallen snow. He stepped out of the helicopter, slamming the door and stalking towards the steps that would lead to the back door of his palace.

He didn't know who'd dared to breach his sanctuary, but he would tell them to leave, in no uncertain terms. Thirio Skartos was not in the mood for being nice.

To say Lucinda Villeneuve was nervous would be an understatement. Not just because she'd arrived uninvited to the castle of a famously reclusive billionaire, proposal in hand, but because of what that proposal meant to her. If he agreed to hire her as the events coordinator for his sister's wedding, it would truly change Lucinda's life. The fee alone would be enough to secure a bank loan, so that she could finally buy out her awful stepmother and regain control of her late father's business. And more than that, it would prove to her doubters exactly what Lucinda was capable of.

She *had* to convince him that she was the woman for the job.

There wasn't a lot of information about Thirio Skartos on the Internet. Up to a point, there were tons of photographs: a young, handsome partyboy bachelor who seemed to go from one event to another—she was familiar with the type. But when tragedy struck and his parents were killed in a house fire, he disappeared from the public eye. For the last six years, he'd almost faded from existence, so it took some sniffing around for Lucinda to secure the address of his hideaway here in the Alps, on the border of Switzerland, France and Italy.

His younger sister, Evie, was easier to research. While she kept a low profile, she'd recently become engaged to the Prince of Nalvania, the fourth son of the reigning monarch, and so there'd been a spate of interviews. Lucinda had spent weeks analysing them, studying them, learning what she could about the soon-to-be Princess and weaving those titbits into her proposal. She *knew* it was good. Great, in fact. She just had to convince Thirio Skartos of that.

If he ever turned up!

Having arrived at the castle some hours earlier, she'd waited in her car a while, before moving into the foyer of the house and then, finally, going a little deeper, when the tea she'd had on the drive up had caught up with her and she'd needed to relieve herself. Only the search for amenities had taken her past the most stunning library, with triple-height ceilings and walls lined with ancient books. Was there really any harm in waiting for him there? She had decided not, and so it was here, in the library, curled up in an armchair with a very old copy of *War and Peace* in her hands, that Thirio discovered her.

Lucinda wasn't sure what she'd been expecting. His good looks were well established. She'd seen photographs of him online, taken years earlier, with his swarthy complexion, eyes darker than night, brows thick and straight, nose aquiline, jaw square—but the man who strode into the library looking as though he wanted to strangle something or someone was very, very different. Oh, his face showed the relics of that handsome young man, but his expression was so angry, so serious, that it was impossible to reconcile him with the smiling, carefree bachelor. And he was such a man—all six and a half feet of steel and strength; there was a darkness to his energy that was overpowering. Lucinda scrambled to her feet, thrusting the book guiltily onto the armchair, all professionalism forgotten in the face of Thirio's overt masculinity.

'Who the hell are you?' His accent was crisper than the temperature outside. His father was Greek, his mother Swiss, and he'd been educated between London and Vienna. He sounded as though he could pass for a member of the British royal family. But his voice was rough, thick and hoarse, as though he didn't use it often. As though he was angry to be using it now.

Lucinda swallowed past a bundle of nerves.

'Thirio Skartos?'

'You are in my house,' he said succinctly. 'Do you think you have any right to ask questions of me?'

She had not expected this degree of animosity. 'I have been trying to contact you via phone,' she responded haughtily, forgetting for a moment how badly she needed his business. 'You haven't returned my calls.'

'Most people would take that as a hint.'

'I'm not most people.'

His nostrils flared as he crossed his arms over his chest, staring at her wordlessly, so Lucinda's pulse ratcheted up without warning, without explanation. She bit down on her lower lip, then quickly stopped, when his very dark eyes dropped to the gesture, slowly appraising it, and then, her face.

'You are not welcome here.'

'I just need a moment of your time.'

Scepticism tightened his face. 'Do you not understand English?'

Lucinda flinched. He was not the first person to question her intelligence. Ever since her father had died, her stepmother and stepsisters had peppered her with insults, constantly undermining and taunting her.

What this man didn't understand was that Lucinda had learned to be strong in the face of putdowns, even when it took an immense effort.

'I appreciate what you're saying,' she conceded

after a slight pause. 'But I don't intend to go anywhere until we've spoken. If you truly want to be alone, I suggest you listen to me. The sooner you've heard me out, the sooner I can leave.'

She'd surprised him. 'Who do you think you are to come into my home and start delivering ultimatums? I could have you arrested.'

'You could,' she confirmed with a slight nod, trembling inwardly. 'But that would take longer and involve more people. Whereas I don't intend to stay a moment longer than this conversation requires.'

It was very obvious that Thirio Skartos was not used to being challenged. If Lucinda's whole future and livelihood weren't hanging on his acceptance of her proposal, she'd have enjoyed the way his jaw was spasming with the effort of staying calm. It was fun to rile him, and she suspected he needed it. But this was too important—she couldn't go too far.

'I really won't take up much of your time.' She switched to a conciliatory tone of voice. 'It's getting dark and I don't much like the idea of tackling that road in the evening.'

'An excellent point,' he murmured, casting an eye towards the windows. 'And a storm is coming. If I were you, Miss—'

'Lucinda Villeneuve.'

He nodded once. Despite having prompted her for her name, he looked impatient at the interruption. 'I would leave while you still can. I'm going to take a shower.'

Lucinda's jaw dropped. Well, that had backfired spectacularly. She had very little information on this man, but one thing had stood out to her when she'd been doing her research. His sister spoke glowingly of him. She guessed their relationship to be close-knit.

'So you don't care what I came here to say?'

'Isn't that obvious?'

'Despite it involving your sister?'

Thirio paused. 'What about her?' Every word was sharpened like a bullet.

Lucinda took a step closer, then wished she hadn't, when a hint of his masculine aroma reached her nostrils. He wore a cologne that was all citrus spice, but beneath it there was a muskiness that was all him. This time, her response was unmistakable. Desire snaked in the pit of her stomach. She stopped walking and planted her feet firmly on the parquet floor of the library.

'Your sister is getting married and you're responsible for organising the wedding.'

There was a slight pause, as though he was going to argue. 'Did you come here to state the obvious?'

Again, a flicker of hurt lashed Lucinda. Not because of this man's words but because of words she'd heard far too many times in her twenty-five years.

'I believe I can give your sister her dream wedding.'

'You and every events coordinator from here to Sydney,' he responded with a curl of his lips that only made Lucinda more determined.

'The difference is, I'm right.'

She turned and walked towards a stunning carved table beneath a large window that overlooked a densely wooded forest. 'I know you'd agree if you'd take ten minutes to review my plans.'

'Wedding planning submissions are to be sent over email.'

'I know that.'

'So why are you here?'

Because I desperately need this job. 'My proposal is too big for email.'

'Then you should hone it further and submit it when you're done. I don't have time to read thirty pages of nonsense because you have difficulties being succinct.'

She gasped. 'You really are—'

'Yes?' he demanded, holding her eyes. Her heart thumped, and her knees felt all tingly.

She pulled back her own temper. 'What reason could you possibly have for refusing to listen?'

'How's this? I want to be alone.'

She flinched, curiosity and, strangely, sympathy washing through her. But this was too important for Lucinda to be put off.

'Okay.' She lifted her hands appeasingly. 'I promise, I'll leave. But first, let me describe—quickly—the dream wedding I've planned for her.'

'It's a wedding,' he growled. 'She'll wear a big white dress, he'll wear a tuxedo, there'll be a band and food and alcohol and, at the end of it all, they'll be married.'

'Why the heck did your sister put you in charge if that's how you feel about these things?'

He opened his mouth as if to respond and then closed it again. 'That's not your concern.' He turned and walked towards the doors of the library. 'I presume you can see yourself out?'

Lucinda stared at him, open-mouthed. 'Will you at least promise to review the plan?' She held up the information, neatly collated into a booklet. Contrary to his implication, the data was succinct, the plans tightly worded to convey the effect of her intentions without getting bogged down in the minutiae of planning. That, after all, would be her job.

'No.' The single word reverberated through the castle and then he disappeared. His broad back fascinated her until he turned the corner and disappeared—taking with him all the hopes and fantasies Lucinda had created of Evie Skartos's dream wedding. Especially the freedom it would finally grant to her.

He stripped out of his clothes gratefully, as though each item he removed was also relieving him of the day's work, of the meetings he'd sat through, the deferential sympathy he'd endured, the curiosity, the watchfulness, the speculation. Did they think he didn't hear the whispering? Did they think he didn't know what it meant?

Naked in his bathroom, he let his eyes fall to the floor-to-ceiling mirror, inspecting his body slowly. At first, he'd hated the scars that started on his left flank and rose over his hip then bloomed beneath his arm to cover one pectoral muscle and the edge of his back, then higher, to his neck and the base of his throat. He'd hated them because they were a constant reminder, and now he relished them for that exact reason. His body bore the marks of his guilt, and he was glad.

The scars were a way of making sure he would never forget. Not that there was much danger of that—his mother's screams were embedded in his brain and could never be dislodged—but the scarring ensured he thought of that night often. Several times a day. He relived the trauma, and he replayed his part in it, the guilt he bore because he'd been a stupid, drunken fool.

He ran his fingers over the torn flesh, and, out of nowhere, pictured *her* fingers. The woman who'd dared to invade his space, to walk into his home and act as though he owed her anything. When she'd lifted that bloody folder, he'd noticed that her hands were delicate and pale, her nails short and rounded, her skin like porcelain. As his finger travelled the length of his scarring, the matted sensation familiar to him, he imagined her hands travelling the length, touching him like this, feeling the scar, her wide, amber-coloured eyes following the trajectory of the damage, her lips— He groaned, because her lips had been impossible to ignore. Perfect pillows of pink, with a Cupid's bow and a quickness to smile, even when he was glowering at her. He'd wanted to reach out and rub his thumb over them, to feel them part at his touch, and her warm breath escape, curling around his wrist. He'd wanted—

But he no longer deserved those pleasures. He had vowed never to indulge them again: celibacy was small penance, given his crime. He had stolen from his parents the chance to live their lives, he had no business taking joy in his.

For six years, he'd existed in self-imposed purgatory. He had not missed his old life, and the luxuries that came with it. He hadn't missed partying, alcohol, women, laughter. He hadn't missed anything except his parents, and the life he'd so foolishly taken for granted for so long.

When he thought of *that* life, and how spoiled he'd been, Thirio wanted to become a boy again, a boy who could curl up into a ball and cry in the corner, a boy who could scramble onto his mother's lap and be told that everything would be okay. But Thirio was not a boy and he knew nothing would ever be okay again. It was simply a matter of existing, for Evie's sake, and never allowing himself to forget all the reasons he had for turning his back on pleasure and life.

But he was still human.

He was still a man.

And he was still capable of feeling. Of temptation. Unbidden, his eyes strayed to the window. His legs followed, carrying him towards it, until his eyes fell on her.

He wouldn't have said he had a type of woman. Before the explosion and fire, Thirio had known only that he liked women—a lot. Tall, short, slim, curvaceous, blonde, brunette, he didn't much care. But instinctively he knew this woman was *not* his type. Oh, she was very beautiful, with her dark blonde hair that tumbled down her shoulders in luxurious waves, and eyes that were the colour of sun-warmed honey, clear, almost pearlescent skin and a slim, toned figure that he'd been unable to avoid noticing, given that she wore a form-fitting turtleneck and black trousers. Yes, she was beautiful, but she was also young, sweet and somehow fragile, so that even when he'd been barking at her to get the hell out of his house, he'd felt a strange desire to protect her.

Ridiculous.

Thirio was nobody's saviour, and she was, technically, a criminal. Breaking and entering was still considered illegal, wasn't it?

As he watched, she paused, turning to regard

the castle, and the late afternoon sun bounced off her face, so she almost appeared to shimmer, like a fairy-tale princess. But there was no such as thing as fairy tales. Her eyes travelled the turrets, the wonderment on her features unmistakable.

He didn't move. In fact, he stood as still as an ancient statue, and yet, somehow, her eyes shifted quickly, as if drawn to his window, to *him*. It was impossible to know how much she could see. After all, these windows were old and rippled and the sun would surely be creating a reflection of the forest. And yet her eyes lingered. Inexplicably, he remained right where he was, his torn, broken body defiantly visible, as if challenging her to look at him like the wide-eyed ingenue she'd been downstairs.

Christos, she was beautiful.

The thought resonated through his brain so fast it was like a whip cracking, and a moment later, there was lightning—not inside his mind, though he felt that too, but beyond the ridge of the forest, cutting through the darkening sky like a blade.

The storm was approaching much faster than forecast.

Muttering a curse, he turned away from the window and grabbed his jeans, his lips a grim line in his face. She couldn't drive down the mountain in these conditions. For anyone, the road would be perilous, but for someone who wasn't familiar with the terrain, it was an accident waiting to happen, and Thirio had known enough of accidents and death for a lifetime.

CHAPTER TWO

THE ENGINE TURNED over with a delightful purr, so Lucinda closed her eyes and said a small prayer of gratitude. Mortification was heating her cheeks. Coming here had been a huge mistake. It had been bad enough to invade his personal space, but to *stare* at his half-naked—possibly even fully naked!—body? Unforgivable.

She flicked the car into drive, eager to escape. A quick glance in her rear-vision mirror and Lucinda was about to pull out, only a swift movement caught her eye.

Thirio.

Half dressed, still, his torso immediately drawing her attention. All of it. Every single iota of focus fell on his flesh, so sculpted and strong, so bronzed, and scarred on one side. Her heart thumped heavily against her ribs, making it almost impossible to breathe.

He stalked towards her quickly, a look on his face that was as thunderous as the clouds overhead.

As he approached the vehicle she forced her

brain to connect to her body, and wound down the window. 'Yes?'

'You cannot leave.'

'Why not?'

'The storm will be here within minutes.' As if nature wanted to underscore his point, another bolt of lightning split the sky in two; a crack of thunder followed. 'You won't make it down the mountain.'

Lucinda's eyes slashed to the gates that led to the castle and, beyond them, the narrow road that had brought her here. Even in the sunshine of the morning, the drive had been somewhat hair-raising. She didn't relish the prospect of skiing her way back down to civilisation.

She turned to look at him, but that was a mistake, because his chest was at eye height, and she wanted to stare and lose herself in the details she saw there, the story behind his scar, the sculpted nature of his muscles. Compelling was an understatement.

'So what do you suggest?' she asked carefully.

'There's only one option.' The words were laced with displeasure. 'You'll have to spend the night here.'

'Spend the night,' she repeated breathily. 'Here. With you?'

'Not with me, no. But in my home, yes.'

'I'm sure I'll be fine to drive.'

'Will you?' Apparently, he saw through her

claim. 'Then go ahead.' He took a step backwards, yet his eyes remained on her face and, for some reason, it almost felt to Lucinda as though he were touching her.

Rain began to fall, icy and hard. Lucinda shivered.

'I—you're right,' she conceded after a beat. 'Are you sure it's no trouble?'

'I didn't say that.'

His tone made her flinch. He was truly the most unpleasant man she'd ever met, despite his physical appeal.

'Maybe the storm will clear quickly.'

'Perhaps by morning.'

'Perhaps?'

'Who knows?'

The prospect of being marooned in this incredible castle with this man for any longer than one night loomed before her. Anticipation hummed in her veins.

'Now, can we go inside before I freeze to death?'

Of course! He was shirtless and the rain icy. She nodded, putting her window back up and turning off the engine of the car. In those precious few seconds, Lucinda tried to pull herself together. Ever the optimist, she realised that a night with Thirio Skartos at least gave her an opportunity to make him listen to her proposal. She'd worked so hard on it; she was sure that if he heard what she had planned, he'd want her to organise the wedding.

But was that just a fool's hope? Because she could finally see a way to get rid of her step-mother and stepsisters and save her father's company. Nothing meant more to Lucinda than that. He had built it from scratch and she wanted to honour her father's memory. She'd finally take her place as his heir, and run things as he once had, restoring prestige to the company that was waning every day her stepmother was at the helm.

Evie Skartos's wedding was the key to that.

Determination fired through Lucinda, pushing everything else from her mind. Well, almost everything. It was hard not to acknowledge a tremor of sensual awareness when she pushed out of the car and came within a few inches of her unwitting host.

'Do you have a bag?' His tone could not be less welcoming, but the question itself showed a degree of thoughtfulness that surprised her. So too his concern for her safety, come to think of it. Maybe he wasn't all bad?

'No,' she said with regret. 'It's in a hotel in the city.'

His curt nod gave nothing away. He turned, striding back to the castle and holding the door open for her. She stared at it for several seconds, her throat inexplicably dry, before she stepped into the hall, almost brushing him as she passed.

He was warm. They hadn't touched and yet somehow she just felt it. Her skin seemed to be heating as if in response.

'Thank you,' she managed to murmur, then almost wished she hadn't offered the civility, for the way his face shifted, rejecting her gratitude.

'Follow me.' She wasn't sure how he managed to inject three syllables with so much disdain, but he did so with apparent ease. Little did he know, she'd had a lifetime of being treated like dirt by her supposed family—his behaviour didn't really phase her after that.

She fell into step just behind him, giving more attention to the castle now. The storm added a haunted, ethereal elegance to the rooms; the candelabras, while beautiful in the full daylight, were quite spectacular in the brooding, moody light.

'How long have you lived here?'

He stopped walking, but didn't turn to face her. His shoulders were tense. 'Rule number one. You are not my guest. You are not my friend. I have no interest in making small talk with you.' He turned slowly. 'And I certainly have no interest in answering questions. In case I have not made it obvious, you are here for one reason only: I do not want your death on my conscience.' The words reverberated with the strength of steel. 'The kitchen is through there.' He gestured to a pair of timber doors to his right. 'Eat whatever you want. But just…' He broke off, his eyes searching hers, the smallest of frowns arching between his brows before he seemed to rouse himself. 'Stay out of my goddamned way.'

She did exactly as he asked. For several hours, Thirio didn't hear a peep from his unwanted visitor. But he *knew* she was there. He could *feel* her in the castle, he could sense her. Vitally, he knew he wasn't alone, and being solitary was all he craved, particularly after the day he'd had.

His mind ran over the meeting he'd run, focusing on the details, but every few minutes a pair of amber eyes flooded his mind. So, some time after eight, he left the sanctuary of his office and began to stalk through the castle. He wasn't looking for Lucinda specifically, and yet, when he found her in the library, he was glad. Just to know what she was up to, to convince himself that she wasn't sticking her nose where it wasn't wanted. Thirio valued his privacy almost as much as he did his solitude.

'Hello.' Her voice was soft. Sweet. He ignored the tightening in his gut, the feeling that shifted through him that there was more to this diminutive, gentle woman. Curiosity was normal. Thirio didn't see many people. He even tended to speak to Evie on the phone or via WhatsApp, rather than face to face. He couldn't bear his sister's kindness, nor the sympathy that softened the corners of her eyes.

'Have you eaten?'

Her brows flexed together at the harshness of his tone. He told himself he was glad. Better that she be wary of him than look at him with sensual speculation. 'I grabbed an apple.'

'That's not dinner.'

'It's fine. I don't tend to eat much at night anyway. I'm usually so busy, I just have something quick.' She frowned softly. 'You don't have to worry about me.'

'I'm not,' he rejected that idea, but too quickly. The words didn't ring true. He expelled a rough breath. 'As I said, I don't want your death on my conscience. Come with me.' He stalked out of the room without checking that she was following. It had been a long time since Thirio Skartos was with people, but he still carried the belief that he would always be obeyed, always be followed.

'I don't think I'm going to die from starvation.' Her voice lifted in amusement and it did something strange to him. Something unwelcome, for the sheer fact of how good it felt.

'Probably not.' So why was he doing this? Why was he leading her to the kitchen, as though she were an invited guest rather than an opportunistic gatecrasher?

He pushed through the double doors, frustrated by the uncharacteristic behaviour. He supposed it was the novelty of having someone here. *And the fact she's as beautiful as an angel has nothing to do with it? The fact your libido is stirring to life for the first time in six years?* He ground his teeth together, wrenching open the freezer door and withdrawing two ready-prepared meals.

'Lasagne okay?'

She wrinkled her nose. 'I'm…'

'What?'

His curt interruption startled her. She visibly jumped and regret twisted his gut. He was all hard edges now, nothing soft about him.

'I'm a vegetarian.' The words emerged as an apology, and he felt even worse. For Christ's sake. He'd forgotten how to be around another human.

He replaced the lasagnes and removed, instead, a couple of portions of mushroom risotto.

'No problem.' He didn't look up to see her response, but instead busied himself with putting the contents into the microwave.

'Drink?'

She shook her head, her long, dark blonde hair shifting around her face.

Regardless of her answer, he removed a vintage bottle of wine from a special fridge and poured two glasses.

She eyed hers uncertainly. 'I really am sorry to have inconvenienced you.'

She hadn't. Not really. Her being here was a nuisance because he hated people—*all people*—but she hadn't personally done anything to exacerbate that.

'Why did you come here?'

'I told you. I wanted to talk to you about—'

'My sister's wedding. I don't mean that.' He lifted his wine glass to his lips, savouring the flavour before replacing it on the benchtop. 'Do you fly internationally to pitch for every event you want to manage?'

'This isn't just any event,' she pointed out, reaching for her own glass and taking a delicate sip, her full pink lips pressing against the glass in a way he found he couldn't ignore, her pale throat shifting as she swallowed. His gut tightened, muscles low down in his abdomen clenching with speculation and long-repressed need.

'I see. So my sister's reputation is why you're here.'

She hesitated, her eyes roaming his face for several seconds before she focused on a point over his shoulder. 'Actually, your sister is.'

'Do you know Evie?'

'Not personally, no. But there was something she said in her engagement interview that made me want to handle her wedding myself.'

'Not because she's marrying a prince and the budget is unlimited?' He couldn't help prodding, sure that the enormous chunk of money he'd pay out to the successful events firm had something to do with Lucinda's persistence.

'I mean, obviously that's part of it,' she agreed. 'To have a client for whom money is no object means the sky's the limit with the arrangements, but actually, no. That's not it.'

'So why, then?'

'Because I'm an orphan too,' she said, so softly he almost didn't catch the words. Her eyes were soft, her lips pursed as if she were lost in thought. 'My mother died when I was a baby. I never knew her. My father and I were very close, but I lost him when I was just fifteen.' She swallowed, and again, his eyes dropped to her throat, where the muscles bunched together. 'When your sister spoke of your parents, and how she wanted to feel them with her on her wedding day, I just knew I'd be the right person for this job, because I understand what that's like. I understand what it's like to live each day fully aware that there's this huge gap in your heart, that won't ever close over.' She lifted her slender shoulders, but Thirio was no longer looking at her. His ears were ringing with a familiar pressure, his breathing coming in short rasping spurts. Panic. He was on the brink of a panic attack. And this woman would witness it. He turned away quickly, staring at the microwave, focusing on his breathing. In, out. In, out. He closed his eyes but there were his parents, his mother's smile, his father's laugh. And then there were their voices, the screams his mother had made right up until smoke had filled her lungs and taken her away.

All because of him.

'I will consider your proposal with the others.'

His voice sounded surprisingly normal. The timer dinged; he plated their meals and placed them on the counter.

'Or…' she dragged the word out, her tone flirtatious without, he suspected, her intending it to be '…we could discuss it now. Pretty please. It won't take long, and I promise, you'll be glad. When you hear what I've put together, I know you'll be convinced this is a good fit.'

'You really don't give up, do you?'

'No. And that's another reason you should want me on the job.'

'Generally, I admire persistence,' he admitted after a beat. 'But I'm not in the mood tonight.'

'Or ever?' she prompted, watching carefully as he garnished their meals with a drizzle of olive oil.

'What does that mean?'

'You don't seem like the wedding planning type. Why did your sister put you in charge?'

It was a question he didn't feel like answering. 'Remember rule number one?'

She blinked, confusion on her features so beautiful and surprising that he wanted to take the words back. 'I'm not your house guest,' she said softly. 'Meaning you don't want to answer the question?'

'There is no question to answer.' His nostrils flared. 'You really are very inquisitive for someone who turned up on my doorstep uninvited.'

'Hey.' Her voice held a reprimand, which he wasn't expecting. 'You started this.' Her eyes were reproachful, and he felt that all the way to his gut. He hardened himself to her obvious charms.

'I feel I have the right to ask *you* questions,' he responded, spooning some rice into his mouth and glaring at her as he ate.

'You're wrong.' She jutted her chin out defiantly. 'You have no rights over me. The fact that I'm here doesn't mean I have to answer your questions, any more than you have to answer mine.'

'You don't think so?'

'No.' She pushed the risotto away. 'I've lost my appetite.'

He arched a brow. 'A hunger strike?'

Despite her obvious irritation, her lips quirked, a small smile slipping past her guard. His gut kicked. He liked seeing her smile. Danger sirens blared. He ate some more of his own dinner. 'Answer the question and I'll eat,' she bartered.

He moved the bowl closer to her, then crossed his arms.

'I'm good with details—wedding or otherwise.' And at this moment, he was noticing far too many details about the woman opposite him.

'So am I,' she said after a small pause. 'I've put a lot of work into the details for the wedding. I know it's what she'd want.'

Her confidence was seductive. 'And I'll consider your plan; I've told you that.'

'With the other proposals?'

'Did you seriously think turning up here in person, uninvited, would confer special privileges on your bid?'

Heat flushed her cheeks, so they were the exact same shade as her lips. He watched, fascinated, as the colour spread, imagining her strawberries and cream complexion beneath her turtleneck. Wondering if her breasts would be this same shade, and her nipples a dusty pink.

His groin strained against his jeans and he was glad then for the height of the bench. He really was out of practice if he was getting a hard-on just looking at a woman.

'Yes, actually.' She jabbed her dinner. 'Most people would appreciate the fact I've literally gone the extra mile.'

'I didn't ask for applications to be sent via email so that my request could be ignored. To be honest, the fact that you showed up here works against you. Big time. I'm not going to hire anyone who doesn't respect my requests. I'm not interested in arguing with the events company I hire. When I specify a way of doing business, I expect that to be adhered to.'

'You mean obeyed,' she quipped swiftly, sipping her wine, as though the drink could cool down her cheeks.

'Fine, obeyed. Is there a problem with that?'

'Well, how many events do you organise a year?'

He stared at her coldly. 'Your point?'

'That you don't know what you're doing.'

He resisted the strong temptation to point out that he single-handedly oversaw several multi-billion-dollar enterprises. 'I see. Is this how you usually go about ingratiating yourself with prospective clients?'

'I don't flatter anyone to gain work,' she responded swiftly. 'I'm honest. That's part of my charm.'

He didn't want to dwell on her charms, even when certain parts of his anatomy could think of little else.

'You need someone at the helm of this who knows what they're doing, and that's not you.'

He almost laughed at her assertion, but it had been so long, Thirio suspected he'd forgotten how. He drank his wine instead.

'How many events like this do *you* organise each year, then?'

For someone who'd been putting him in his place a moment earlier, she went very, very quiet.

'What? Cat suddenly got your tongue?'

Her cheeks went bright pink. He pressed his hands into the benchtop to stop from the sudden, almost irresistible urge to reach out and feel the heat for himself. What if she wasn't real? If he was going to conjure up someone to distract himself from his nightmare reality, then this woman would be exactly it.

'I—'

Her eyes dropped to the food.

Something sparked in his chest. Suspicion. Desire had muddled his senses but now instincts were returning. 'You're hiding something from me.'

Her eyes flicked to his, guilt obvious in their honey depths. Her hand lifted then, searching for something at her throat. She pulled down the roll-neck of her sweater and found a small necklace— a diamond on a silver chain, pulling the pendant from one side to the other. A tell, if ever he'd known one.

He waited.

'Technically, I don't usually do this kind of thing at all.'

He stared at her, the admission catching him completely off guard. 'What kind of thing?'

'Any of this.' She took a long sip of wine, then placed the glass down, tinkering with the stem.

His eyes narrowed. 'Turn up at people's houses and walk in uninvited?'

'Well, that too.' She gnawed on her lower lip. Yearning spread through him like a tidal wave. He could barely remember what it was like to lose himself in a woman, her soft curves and un-dulations, to feel her warmth surrounding him. His groin tightened to the point of pain. His face gave nothing away.

'Technically, I'm not an events planner.'

His gaze narrowed. 'Then what are you?'

There was a plea in her eyes, one that very nearly weakened him. But Thirio wasn't interested in being this woman's saviour. It just wasn't within his skill set. He sipped his wine and waited silently.

'I'm an administrative assistant for an event management company.' The words were drenched in bitterness. She blinked, as if to clear whatever ungenerous thought had darkened her mind for a moment. 'The company I work at was my father's. I grew up in the office, learning the ropes from him. But when he died...' her voice faltered, and her eyes shifted away '...my stepmother took over.'

'And she hired you to do the administrative work.'

Her lips pressed together, as though she was biting back her first response. He didn't want that though. He didn't welcome secrecy.

He had no patience for lies. 'I deserve to know the truth.'

'Because I offended you by coming here in person?'

'Because you're lobbying to coordinate my sister's wedding. And if I was going to hire you, I'd need to know I could trust you.'

'You can.' Her eyes almost pierced him with their intensity. She appraised him slowly, as if evaluating him, and finally lifted her shoulders, as if in surrender. 'My stepmother gave me the administrative responsibilities because I'm good at that. I'm great at making our office run like clockwork. But I'm even better at people. I'm good at reading them, great at delivering for them. I genuinely care about our clients. She doesn't realise how much I do behind the scenes, how many events I've coordinated without her looking. I promise, I will deliver your sister the wedding she never dared dream of.'

He stared at her long and hard, wondering if she could feel the crackle in the air around them. Wondering if she was just very adept at ignoring it, and other things too, such as if she had a boyfriend, a lover, a husband? If Thirio hadn't sworn to abstain from pleasure, from anything that could bring him happiness he didn't deserve, he would have acted on the feelings that were rioting through him. He'd have leaned closer and let his breath brush her ear, his body lightly touching hers. He would have made it obvious that he was trying to inhale her sweet, vanilla scent, or fantasizing about throwing her over his shoulder and carrying her to his bedroom…

But Thirio had denied himself so much for so long that, despite the temptation that had walked into his home, he had no intention of weakening now.

'Please, Thirio. I need this.'

Despite the softness of her words, the sentiment

cracked around the room like a whip, drawing him in. His name on her lips was an aphrodisiac. His control was in the balance.

And so he fought back hard now, while he still could.

'My sister's wedding is not a charity. I won't give you the job just because you beg.'

CHAPTER THREE

IT WAS IMPOSSIBLE not to regret her impetuosity in setting out for Castile di Neve in that moment. But ever since her father's death, she'd been told she wasn't good enough, even when she knew she was. For years, Lucinda had put up with the demeaning low-level jobs her stepmother had doled out, while watching her stepsisters attempt to keep the blue-chip roster of clients her father had cultivated. Didn't they realise how disastrous things would be if Lucinda hadn't kept intervening? If she hadn't made phone calls in the evenings to smooth over the mishaps? If she hadn't checked and triple-checked every detail until it was assured each engagement would run perfectly?

And now, for the first time in years, she could see a way out of this mess. If only Thirio would listen to her plans.

'I'm not asking you for charity,' she corrected with quiet strength. 'I just want you to consider my proposal.'

'I have said that I intend to.'

'I mean, now.'

'Before there's any competition from other companies?'

'There is no competition,' she said immediately, with more than bravado, because Lucinda knew that the wedding she'd planned was beyond spectacular. Exceeding a client's needs was her goal in life, just as it had been her father's. 'My plan is best. I'm only trying to save you time.'

'How magnanimous of you.' The cynicism was palpable.

'You really don't like me, do you?'

His dark eyes bored into hers, showing surprise at the honest question. 'Frankly, you're irrelevant. But I've made it clear, I don't look kindly on anyone invading my space as you have.'

She couldn't help but stare. She knew he'd been through a lot—losing his parents as he had—but that didn't give him a free pass to treat people like this.

She took a forkful of the risotto, and then another, and another, until her bowl was finished.

'That was delicious, thank you.' Her voice was stiff and formal, reminding her of how she interacted with her family. Not that they were her real family—just people she'd been thrown together with when her father had died. At fifteen, she'd been too young to be cut loose, but by eighteen, she'd been far too useful to let go.

So why hadn't *she* left? Why hadn't she walked

away when her stepmother's treatment had become increasingly worse?

Because that would have meant leaving behind her family home, and her father's legacy, something she could never imagine. So she stayed and she toiled despite being treated like garbage day in, day out. But a flicker of something like rebellion ran through her now. Enough was enough.

'You know, I really didn't plan this.'

'I didn't say that you did.'

'No, but you're acting as though I came here looking to inconvenience you and I can assure you that's not the case. I had no idea you'd take my presence as some kind of insult, but if I'd known you'd feel this way, believe me, I would have avoided the trip.'

He pushed aside his own bowl, bracing his palms on the counter and regarding her with that steady, dark stare. 'You're here. There's no point arguing about why now. If you've had enough to eat, I'll show you to your room.'

But anger was coursing through her. An anger that wasn't really his fault, an anger that didn't sit at his feet alone. It had been building inside her for years, and now, in this unexpected circumstance, it washed over her like a crushing tidal wave.

'Thank you,' she bit out, doing her best not to snap, not to argue, when her insides were churning at the injustice of his treatment. Okay, this clearly wasn't ideal. She shouldn't have come, she shouldn't have let herself in. She could see that was a misstep. But he was the one who'd insisted she stay. He was the one who'd chased after her and offered her his home for the night.

Yeah, to stop you driving over the edge of the cliff in the middle of a bad snowstorm. Not because he was yearning for your company. The heat of her anger faded, leaving her with a strange empty feeling in the pit of her stomach. It was far too reminiscent of the way she'd felt for years. Unwanted. Surplus to requirements.

As a teenager, she'd learned that disappearing into her room was best. She'd kept a low profile in the hope of avoiding conflict, and it seemed like the best course of action now. If only she knew where she'd be sleeping tonight.

'I—' She opened her mouth to pose the question, but Thirio beat her to it, speaking at the exact same moment.

'I will give you ten minutes to go through it,' he said with a darkness to his voice that made her insides squirm.

'Really?'

'Really.' He crossed his arms over his chest and despite the fact he was wearing a shirt now, she saw him without and, suddenly, she could hardly think straight. Her mind went fuzzy.

'Um, do you mind if I make a coffee?' There was so much at stake. She had to nail this.

His nostrils flared as he exhaled. 'How do you take it?'

'Just black.'

His lips curled with an emotion she couldn't place and then his magnificent back was to her, broad and powerful, as he brought a fancy-looking machine to life and began to brew two coffees. Hers was in an ordinary-size cup, his a short black, just the essence of coffee.

'Go.'

Nervous butterflies filled her belly. She took a deep breath, summoning her professional experience and the plan she'd been slaving over for weeks.

'Your sister has spoken about this castle often, you know. As a teenager, before the accident,' she offered with a sympathetic grimace, the pain of losing your parents one with which Lucinda was familiar, 'she was interviewed by one of those teen magazines and she mentioned family holidays here. I know it's very special to her.'

Thirio's expression was inscrutable but something in his eyes made the butterflies in her tummy double in number.

'And it's such a spectacular venue. I knew as soon as I saw a picture that it would be just perfect.'

Silence crackled around them.

'Perfect for what?' he asked, his casual tone forced, so she knew that tension underpinned it.

Okay. This was going to take work. 'The wedding.' She rushed on before he could argue. 'In my plan, I have overcome every objection you could make. The logistics of transporting guests from the town to here, the accommodation that could be offered, the caterers. I saw from some photographs online that there's a ballroom. Your sister and her fiancé have said they want an intimate—'

'No.' He held up a hand, silencing her with that one word and gesture. But for good measure, he added, enunciating slowly, 'Absolutely not.'

She'd expected this. Not when she'd first arrived, certainly, but from almost the moment he'd returned home and greeted her like a bear with a hole in his head.

'The private areas of the house would remain cordoned off. We would only grant access to the ballroom indoors, and the chapel outside.'

'There is no chapel outside.'

'There would be, though, made from calico. A large timber floor with a lattice of fairy lights overhead, like a chandelier against the sky. The smell of pine needles filling the space. It will be so incredible. Just what Evie would want.'

His expression bore down on her like a freight train. 'No.'

'Why not?'

'There are one thousand reasons I could give you, but let's go with this one: I don't want strangers in my house.'

'They wouldn't be in your house,' she said slowly. 'I told you, we would keep guests to allotted areas. Your privacy would be protected.'

'No.'

She took in a deep, steadying breath. 'I understand your resistance, but…'

His laugh was short and sharp. 'This proposal is a dead end. If that's all you've got, then you've wasted your time.'

But Lucinda knew he was wrong. Oh, not about his personal wishes, but about what Evie would want.

'Do you agree your sister would want her wedding here?'

He hesitated. 'She would never ask it of me.'

His eyes darkened and he collected his coffee cup, stalking to the kitchen sink and placing it in the bowl, before turning to face her. Bare chest. Scar. Strength. She closed her eyes, willing the images away even when they seemed almost burned into her retina. They didn't help her in this moment.

And then he was walking again, towards the counter, then around it, to stand in front of her. So close she could almost feel the air reverberating with each breath he pushed out. His chest moved, and her stomach twisted. Desire stirred, heating the blood that gushed through her veins.

Focus. Charm him. Change his mind.

'I can show you how it would work.'

'But it won't work.' The words were chilling even when fire seemed to be ravaging her insides. She sucked in a deep breath and tasted him in her mouth. Her belly flopped and she had to clamp her lips together to bite back a soft moan from escaping.

'How do you know?' she challenged, but her tone was husky.

'I just do.'

'That's hardly an answer.'

'It's all the answer I care to give.'

'Even if you're wrong?'

'I'm not,' he snapped.

'I think you are.'

'I'm not sure I care.'

She frowned. 'Would you at least consider it?'

'Not for one iota of a second.'

'Not even to make your sister happy?'

'She's marrying the love of her life. You think the ceremony taking place here is what will make her happy?'

'She deserves the wedding of her dreams,' Lucinda insisted, her own heart heavy with all that she'd lost. 'She wants a wedding that will make her feel as though your parents are with her, watching over her, on this most special day in her life. This place is uniquely special to her. I know I can give her a dream wedding, and I promise to balance that with your need for privacy.'

'You don't know a thing about me or my needs,'

he ground out, somehow closer to her, so now his chest brushed her breasts and her nipples tingled at the unexpected contact, aching against the fabric of her bra. Her eyes fluttered closed and she made a soft sound, a breath that was laced with all the feelings that were pouring through her.

Her own needs were tearing her apart, but they were needs she had no idea how to handle.

'And frankly, you don't know a thing about my sister, either.'

'I've done my research.'

'Apparently not, or you'd have known that this plan was doomed from the start. No wedding will take place at Castile di Neve. Is that clear?'

When she looked into his eyes, her face had to tilt upwards, and they were close enough to kiss. The thought came out of nowhere, impetuous and unwanted but impossible to let go of, so her lips parted and her eyes felt heavy with stars. Desire was a wind rushing through her, warm and inescapable.

'I want—' but Lucinda could barely finish the thought. What she wanted was impossible to articulate, and this man scared her to bits. Not the man himself, but the effect he had on her, and the fact they were here, in this stunning castle, in the middle of a snowstorm.

'What do you want?' The words were a growl.

Neither of them stepped back. It was as if some silent, invisible force had welded them together.

She wanted him to kiss her. She wanted to feel his lips moving over hers, separating them, his tongue lashing hers. She wanted to forget about the wedding of the year, the fee, and what that would mean to her. Most of all, she wanted to forget about her stepmother and the mess she was making of the company, she wanted to forget about her pain and loneliness. She wanted to lose herself, just for one night.

His hand on her cheek seared her flesh. It was light and gentle, the tips of his fingers connecting with the skin beside her eye, at first, and then his whole palm curving around her cheek, while his thumb passed tantalisingly close to her lips. Stars burst through her.

'What do you want?' he repeated, his eyes holding hers, forcing her to stare at him simply because she couldn't look away. It felt as though he were looking into her soul, seeing all the things she usually kept so tightly concealed.

Instead of answering, she swayed forward, closing any gap that had remained between them, so his hardness pressed to her soft curves and something inside her—something vital and unknown—locked into place.

'Answer the question.' His lips were taut, almost white rimmed, and, despite the mask he wore that was carefully muted of emotion, she saw the torment in the depths of his eyes, as though even the hint of this conversation was making him feel things he wished he didn't.

'I don't know,' she whispered.

'Liar.' His response was swift.

'What do I want, then?' she volleyed back, eyes unflinching, heart pounding.

One side of his lip curled, derision unmistakable. 'The same thing I do.'

Dangerous delight soared through her. If she were standing on a precipice, she'd say he'd just given her a push halfway over.

'Which is?'

His eyes sparked with hers and she sucked in a deep breath, right as he dropped his head, his eyes still haunted as his lips covered hers, his mouth taking possession of hers in a way that stole her ability to think and breathe, that made her forget everything she was, everything she'd ever been. For one moment, that moment, there was only this.

'Thirio.' She said his name for no reason other than that he was there, and she liked the way it felt to say it like this, with his tongue sliding into her mouth, twirling with hers. A low, husky moan flooded her throat. She barely knew the man but this one kiss was evoking feelings in her that she'd never known, making her twist and turn with a desire she couldn't contain.

'Tell me what you want,' he commanded into her soul, before breaking the kiss, putting just enough space between them to look into her eyes, but not so much that his lips were far away. Her eyes clung to them, her breath coming in rushed little spurts.

But how could she verbalise it? How could she give voice to the cacophony of wants that were deafening Lucinda from the inside out? Heat spread through her, pinking her cheeks, darkening her eyes, until they were almost the colour of chocolate.

'I—'

Nothing made sense. She'd come here because her father's business's future depended on securing this job, and Thirio was the man in charge of hiring. Yet, at that very moment, Lucinda couldn't say she cared too much about whether her proposal was accepted or not. Other things were so much more important...

'You?' He gave her nothing. He wasn't helping her; he wasn't going easy on her. She closed her eyes, searching for sense, for calm, but, if anything, felt only a greater burden of need. For when her eyes were closed, her other senses were so much sharper, and his proximity set off a cascade of need she was powerless to resist.

'You,' she repeated, a whispered admission rather than a question. She peeked up at him, wondering at the heat that was stirring through her, wondering at the way her temperature was spiking. 'This.'

His own eyes closed then, as though it was the last thing he'd been expecting despite the way they'd just been kissing.

'It's not possible.' The words were heavy, final, and yet he didn't move, so she held her breath, grabbing hold of hope.

It *felt* possible. In that moment, everything she'd ever wanted seemed within her reach.

'You don't know what you're asking of me.'

But she did. Uncertainty with men, insecurity with the opposite sex, had always been a voice in the back of her mind—more often than not, that voice shouted so loudly it crossed over into the front of her mind, so that she never felt anyone would be interested in her. But there was something about Thirio Skartos that overrode those doubts and uncertainties. There was something about the way he looked at her that convinced Lucinda he wanted her right back.

'I think we're asking the same thing of each other.'

His eyes sparked, surprise obvious, and she felt a delicious lick of triumph.

His chest heaved with each breath, his eyes boring into hers, and she lifted a hand, pressing her palm to his chest, feeling the hard and fast rushing of his heart. More triumph flooded her veins.

'I didn't ask you to come here.' His fingers curled around her wrist, holding it right where it was. 'And I don't want to sleep with you.' He pulled her hand from his chest, holding it at their sides, his fingers still wrapped around her flesh, making a mockery of that statement.

'Don't you?'

His eyes closed for the briefest of moments and when he opened them again, she saw a battle being waged in the depths of his eyes. Desire warred with determination.

'No.'

Determination, apparently, won. Rejection seared Lucinda, making her feel like a fool for being so open about her wants, making her feel like an idiot for mistaking the chemistry between them.

'I see.' Pride, thankfully, came to her rescue. She wrenched her arm free and took a step back, somehow managing to summon a smile that was forged in ice. 'I must have misunderstood.'

CHAPTER FOUR

SHE HADN'T MISUNDERSTOOD, THOUGH. She'd read him like a book, and more fool him for not being able to control his responses to her.

After six years, he'd thought his libido had curled up and died. It wasn't as if he hadn't been around a woman in all that time, either. Though he rarely left the castle, when he did, he saw people. Flesh and blood people, beautiful women, who looked at him with the kind of interest he would have, at one time in his life, capitalised on. But Thirio wasn't that man any more.

He'd boxed away that part of his personality, those needs; he'd derived satisfaction from denying himself those pleasures.

And year on year, it had grown easier, so he no longer craved a woman's touch.

The scars on his body reminded him of why he had to abstain, of the loss and destruction he'd caused—not having sex was a very small sacrifice to make, when it came to penance. There was no penance, though, that would ever be enough.

He rolled over in his king-size bed, staring out at the rain lashing his window. It had intensified through the night, so he was glad of one thing: that he had not let her leave the castle.

Instead, the beautiful stranger was in a guest bedroom, just metres from his own.

If he'd had any choice in the matter, Thirio would have installed her on the other side of the castle, just as far away from him as was possible, but most of the place was closed off.

And so, Lucinda was barely twenty feet from him. He muted his breathing, closing his eyes and straining to listen. Was she still awake?

They had barely spoken after his rejection. She'd carried her plate to the sink, he'd muttered for her to leave it. She'd obliged without a word. He'd offered to show her back to her room and they'd walked in stony silence. But that hadn't changed the way the air around them had hummed when they'd crossed the threshold of her room. It hadn't meant he'd been able to easily ignore his body's yearning when he'd eyed the bed, and imagined drawing her into it with him.

And so he'd left before temptation could over-power him.

Thirio didn't deserve the pleasure he knew he'd experience in her arms, and he couldn't take it from her knowing that he would never offer more.

The sooner she left, the better. But for Thirio, the night stretched before him, long and impossible. He flipped onto his side, his eyes finding the silhouette of the pine trees, devouring it restlessly. Morning would come, as it always did, and then, he'd fly her away from here, into the town. Soon, he would be alone again, desire forgotten, opportunity lost, just as he wanted.

The noise was loud and woke her instantly. Lucinda sat up, disorientated and confused. Nothing was familiar. Not the four-poster bed, the renaissance art on the walls, not the view framed by the large bay window, and not the smell of pine and ice that hung in the air.

It took several seconds for Lucinda to remember where she was—and who she was under the same roof as! Just as that memory burst into her consciousness, a rush of ice wind encircled her, so she pulled the duvet higher, looking around. Her door was open.

A shiver ran across her spine. Thirio? Had he—? Surely not.

The sound of howling wind called to her. She pushed back the covers and moved towards the door, the sweater Thirio had given her to sleep in soft across her body. It smelled so good. Freshly laundered with detergent that reminded her of lemons and vanilla. She paused at the door, noting the temperature seemed to drop by several degrees here.

Another noise, this time, the opening of a door.

She turned on instinct, eyes landing on Thirio at the same moment her stomach twisted into a bundle of knots.

Holy crap.

Thirio was shirtless. Again. Only this time, despite the cool of the night, he wore just a pair of grey boxer shorts, so his muscular legs were visible to her very hungry, very fascinated eyes.

Her mouth went dry. Her gaze lifted higher, over his endlessly fascinating chest, marked and beautiful and broad and strong, to his throat, stubbled, and a square jaw that was set in a harsh line of disapproval.

'You should go back to bed.'

'I heard a noise.' Her own voice was barely a whisper. She swallowed to clear her throat.

'A tree came through the window,' he muttered. 'That's all.'

She looked again. One of the magnificent pines had fallen, the tip slicing a path through the large window that she'd been admiring only hours earlier.

She grimaced, the destruction of a no-doubt ancient window a shame to see. 'What can I do to help?'

'Nothing.' His voice was commanding. 'Go back to your room.'

Even then, he was pushing her away, rather than taking her offer of help. She was tempted to argue, to insist on doing something useful, but the set of his jaw showed how little he would welcome argument. None the less, defiance spread through her.

'Rain's lashing the floor. If you get a tarpaulin, I'll help you secure it.'

'I said, go to bed.'

She ground her teeth together. For so long, she'd been told what to do, but with this man, it was different. She supposed her stepmother and sisters had come into her life at a particularly impressionable age, and then, the trauma of her father's death had made it feel impossible to go against her stepmother's wishes. Those habits were so ingrained now, she couldn't imagine fighting them. But with Thirio, everything was new and different and she refused to bend to his will. In fact, she got a thrill out of going against him.

'And I said, I want to help.' She crossed her arms, unaware of the way that simple action pulled the sweater higher, to reveal her slim, toned calves to his obsidian gaze. 'I'm not taking no for an answer.'

His breath hissed between his teeth. 'Fine. Have it your way.'

Pleasure—and power—spread through her.

'Stay here,' he muttered, stalking away from her, towards the wide staircase that led to the lower level. She moved instead to the tree, shivering a little, as the cold spread like icy tentacles through this level of the castle.

He reappeared quickly enough, holding a large

blue sheet of plastic, flicking a light as he went, so the hallway filled with a golden glow. His eyes brushed over her and the frigid temperature in the air seemed to reverse immediately, bathing her in warmth that morphed quickly into lava-like heat. She looked away, face flushed, every part of her vibrating with an awareness that rocked her to the core.

'Grab this.' He held out a corner of the tarp, their fingers brushing as she took hold of it, so lava turned to electricity, bursting from nerve ending to nerve ending. Her eyes flew to his, to find him watching her, his gaze arrested as though he couldn't help himself.

He said something low and soft. A curse, she was sure of it, and then he turned away, taking the other corner of the tarpaulin, over the top of the tree, before approaching the broken window, peering through it.

'How bad is it?'

'The damage looks limited to this window. It could have been much worse.'

'Small mercies,' she agreed, taking a few steps closer to the edge.

'That's enough.' His voice held a warning, so she flicked a glance at him, curiosity shaping her features into an expression of interest.

'I'm just looking.'

'Do you remember why you are here? I do not want your death on my conscience.'

'Then it's just as well I don't intend to die, isn't it?'

'People rarely intend their deaths,' he responded grimly, taking his corner of plastic sheeting and lifting it up, standing taller and threading a piece of rope she'd only just become aware of around the top of the curtain rod. His movements were mesmerising. Steady and sure, confident with an economy of effort that spoke of lithe athleticism. She studied his hands first, capable fingers leading to tanned, smooth wrists and forearms. Then her attention moved to his bare chest and that scar again; she wondered at its origins before her eyes travelled lower, to the shorts that covered his rounded buttocks and muscular legs.

There was such concealed strength in his body, she wondered how he stayed fit. Did he run? Work out? Abseil? How did he spend his time? Their kiss haunted her. Staring at him, she relived the way his mouth had felt on hers, the way he'd tasted, the way he'd dominated her for those brief, beautiful moments, before he'd stepped away and denied them both what they'd wanted.

She wasn't aware of the tarpaulin falling from her fingertips. Her nerve endings were reverberating in awareness and need, but only of this man. The tarpaulin fell to the floor and Thirio angled a glance over his shoulder. Her eyes stayed locked to his fascinating, beautiful chest.

'Have you never seen a scar before?'

She flinched, jerked back to the moment by his darkly mocking words, her eyes finally shifting higher to his eyes, which studied her with barely concealed impatience.

'I wasn't looking at the scar,' she admitted, flushing to the roots of her hair.

'You're a terrible liar.' He pulled hard on the rope, checking it was secure, then strode towards her with a panther's grace and intent. He stood just two feet away from her, one hand on his hip—the side that was unmarked. 'There. Have a proper look. It's just misshapen skin.'

She flinched at his description. She wanted to look away, to tell him she had no interest in him or his scar, but neither was true.

Her eyes holding his, challenging him, she lifted her fingertips, connecting with his marked hip, so his eyes clenched shut and his breath flew from his lungs in one rough exhalation. But he didn't move away. And he didn't ask her to stop. Emboldened, she crept her fingers higher, slowly, so slowly, as if by touching him she could understand, as if he were a sheet of music and she back at her piano, learning to play it. When she reached his ribs, she splayed her fingers wide, trying to capture all of his flesh. She felt the ridges beneath, but didn't stop there. Higher she went, towards his armpit, then detoured out, to his left pectoral muscle, and the hair-roughened nipple. Still watching him, she traced it, her mouth dry, her blood pounding through her veins at how daring she was being. This was so out of character, but it didn't feel at all strange—that was the weirdest thing of all.

'Lucinda.' The word was curt. Taken on its face, it was a warning. But his tone was gravelled and husky, and his heart was thumping, almost as hard as hers. She tilted her chin up, facing him, surprised by how close they stood, how near their mouths were.

'How did it happen?'

His expression was inscrutable, his face a mask that shielded his innermost thoughts. 'A fire.'

'Your parents—' She didn't finish the thought. The words hung between them, the question implicit. Had it been the same fire that had claimed their lives?

'Yes.'

It broke the mood. Thirio stepped sideways, bending down to pick up the dropped tarpaulin, carrying her corner to the other side of the window and reaching up to secure it. She watched his back as he worked, muscles rippling. Desire tightened the walls of her stomach.

'There.' He turned back to face her, his eyes guarded. 'Happy now?'

She wasn't. She was fighting a wave of frustration, and the more she fought it, the more it gnawed at her gut.

'You're wet,' she remarked softly, rather than answering his question.

He lifted a hand to his chest, pressing it to the rain-splashed skin. 'I'll dry.'

She couldn't look away. She wanted him. She wanted him to kiss her, to touch her, she wanted him to take her to bed and make her his in every way. The thought seared her like a lightning bolt. Never in her life had she known such immediate and impulsive desire.

'Thirio.' She said his name then frowned. What she wanted was to issue an invitation, but insecurities she fought so hard to keep at bay reared their heads. He'd already rejected her once, after all.

'Go to bed, Lucinda.' His eyes closed and, for the briefest second, she was sure she saw something strangling his features, something she suspected to be desire. Temptation. 'Now.'

She stood her ground, watching him to see what he would do next. He opened his eyes, realised she wasn't moving and then shook his head slowly. 'Fine, have it your way.' He began to walk, his stride long, and she held her breath, waiting, fingers crossed. But he walked right past her, down the hallway, and into his own room.

Disappointment was a physical ache in the pit of her stomach, the rejection thick and immovable in her soul.

There was nothing for it but to try to sleep, and somehow blot him from her mind.

'Christos.' Thirio tolerated his own room for all of five minutes before throwing back the covers in resignation. The whole level of the castle had been transformed into an ice box. In the time the window was broken, and uncovered, every ounce of warmth had been sucked out, replaced by the arctic air that howled across the Alps. For his own part, he could live with it, but he was conscious of Lucinda in the room just across from his and, for many reasons, he didn't want to subject her to several hours longer in the ice-cold room.

He wrenched open his door, closing the distance between his room and hers, a scowl on his face. He hovered outside her room, strangely uncertain, until he thought of how frigid it was and how freezing she must be, and raised his hand to thump on the door.

'Yes?' Her voice came to him as if from far away. He hesitated a moment, hand on the door-knob, and that unusually tentative gesture brought something like a smile to his face. Since when did Thirio hesitate about anything?

'I'm coming in.'

'Okay.' Again, her voice was distant. When he cracked open the door, he could see why, and his instincts were immediately vindicated. She was huddled under the covers, so that only her eyes peeked out, her flaxen blonde hair like a messy crown. Something kicked in his gut, hard.

'It's too cold to sleep here. Come downstairs.'

'What's downstairs?'

'A fireplace, for one.'

She hesitated, but given the choice between a fridge-like room and the lure of a working fire, she wisely chose the latter.

She pushed back the cover, but when she stood, she drew it with her, wrapping it around her shoulders. The cape might have helped keep her warm but it did little to cover her legs, and it was impossible not to let his eyes flicker lower, just for a moment. It didn't help. Tension wound through him, building in the pit of his stomach, tighter than a spring. He had to conquer this.

Soon, she'd leave. He only had to be strong for a little while longer.

Almost as soon as he'd had the thought, a lightning bolt speared the sky. She flinched, her small gasp doing strange things to his insides. He glanced over his shoulder then wished he hadn't when their eyes met and the air between them charged with electricity.

So much for ignoring her.

He could tolerate her though, and the spark they shared. Just so long as she didn't start talking to him about Evie's wedding, and the preposterous idea of hosting it here. Just so long as she didn't look at him with those amber eyes, and pouting lips. Just so long as she didn't lean close, and breathlessly ask him to kiss her again.

CHAPTER FIVE

LUCINDA STRETCHED LIKE a cat, so warm and cosy that she smiled instinctively, blinking her eyes open slowly, fixing her gaze on the fire across the room, the flames low now, flicking the stack of wood lazily, no longer the frantic, tangling beast that had glowed red in the grate when Thirio had first built it. A different kind of heat built inside her now as she looked around the room, her eyes landing on him asleep in an armchair near the windows that framed another view of the enormous forest that surrounded the castle. The storm had cleared. The sky was still dark, but the rain had stopped, and in the distance she could just see tiny bits of blue peeking through.

Asleep, he was mesmerising. All the tension was gone from his face, so he looked so much more like the young man she'd seen photographs of on the Internet. Carefree and…happy. Her heart skipped a beat, her stomach swished. It felt wrong to stare at him in this unguarded moment, creepy to watch him sleep, and yet she couldn't look away.

Her eyes devoured his face, curiosity driving her actions. Had the fire done this to him? Or was it the death of his parents? Or something else entirely?

'Did nobody ever tell you that it's rude to stare?'

She startled, guilt heating her cheeks as her gaze burst to his to see he was awake, watching her through eyes that were still half shuttered. The tension was back in his features, tightening them to the point of wariness.

'I wasn't staring,' she lied unevenly. And despite the fact the duvet was pulled up to beneath her chin, she felt exposed now, as though he could see right through the fabric and her clothing, to her naked body.

Lucinda had not led a particularly adventurous life. She organised events from behind the scenes and worked tirelessly to support her stepmother and sisters. She did not travel for work; she did not attend the glamorous events herself. This was easily the strangest encounter of her entire life.

'Yes, you were.' He didn't move, and yet he radiated tension, like a cat about to pounce.

'Fine,' she admitted after a beat. 'I was. Is that a problem?'

She'd surprised him. She *loved* surprising him. His eyes widened and his lips shifted, all so quickly it was easy to miss, but then he shrugged his shoulders and, despite the fact he was wearing a dark sweater, she could see him shirtless without any difficulty whatsoever. The image was burned into her retinas.

'I'm not used to it.'

'That's because you live like a recluse.'

A muscle jerked in his jaw. 'You've woken up in a very honest mood.'

'Honesty is my default setting.'

'Is it?' He skimmed her face, frowning, as if trying to understand if she was joking or not.

'You don't believe me? That's ironic.'

A flicker of a smile curved his lips and she realised she liked to see him smiling even more than she liked surprising him. Oh, heaven help her. She was actually *enjoying* being here with him.

It was just the novelty of it. Lucinda had been sheltered all her life. Not by choice—at least, not by her choice. She thought of the few times she'd dated in the past, and her heart was immediately heavy.

'It's also immaterial. After I take you off the mountain, I don't imagine we'll ever see one another again. What I think about you hardly seems to matter.'

Lucinda flinched. It wasn't just his summation of their situation, but his cold delivery. He clearly couldn't wait to see the back of her.

'Let's not forget, you came here under false

pretences, so your claims of honesty seem a little far-fetched.'

'What false pretences, exactly?'

'That you work in event management.'

'I *do* work in event management,' she snapped, pushing the duvet off and sitting up, brushing her hair out of her face simply so she could have something to do with her hands. She had to make him understand.

'As an administrative assistant. That hardly makes you qualified to coordinate my sister's wedding to the Prince of Nalvania.'

Lucinda had been underestimated many times, but, for some reason, hearing that from this man was particularly goading. 'You're wrong. I'm uniquely qualified.'

'Because you are also an orphan?'

She winced. The words were cutting—intentionally so, she was sure of it. He was pushing her away.

'Why are you trying to insult me?'

His gaze dropped to her lips. 'I'm only saying what I've observed.'

'You seem to observe the world through a very cynical film.'

'Do I?'

'I think you know you do.'

One corner of his lips lifted, mockingly.

'I think you were determined not to like me, from the moment you saw me.'

'You had broken into my home,' he pointed out reasonably.

But Lucinda's nerves were stretched to breaking point. 'Not to steal anything,' she said sharply, resisting an urge to roll her eyes—but only just.

'You don't think privacy is a commodity that can be stolen?'

Her heart was thumping inside her chest. Lucinda hated confrontation. She always avoided it. It was one of her superhero skills, to be able to predict when someone's mood was turning and leave the room. She hated it, but with Thirio, she stood her ground regardless, even as her gut was churning and her blood felt as if a tsunami were pounding her from the inside out.

'I believed you'd prioritise your sister's happiness. I was wrong.' She stood, her fingertips tingling. 'I came here, in person, because I needed—' she pressed her teeth into her lower lip. How could she admit to him how much this job would mean to her? How could she explain? And why should she bother? It wouldn't change his mind. 'But that's beside the point.' She forced her eyes to turn to the window, grateful to see the sky was half blue now. 'The storm's clearing. I'll get out of your hair just as soon as I can. Excuse me.'

Her movements were jerky as she walked towards the door. 'You won't be going anywhere.' The words were thrown towards her, dark and commanding. She froze, staring at the door, her pulse in her throat. Slowly, with what she hoped would look like a sense of calm, she turned to face him.

'Oh?'

'The road will be icy, despite the clear sky.'

Lucinda's lips were pursed. 'Well, I can't stay here for ever.'

'Obviously.' His rapid rejoinder pulled at something in her chest. 'I'll check the roads after lunch. If they're clear, you can drive. Otherwise, I'll fly you out.'

Her pulse was hammering in her throat. She felt a thousand and one things, none of them easy to comprehend. How could she feel alight with desire even when she hated so much about this man?

'We can use the time to discuss the wedding,' she said after a beat, her arms crossed over her chest as she stared at him.

He stood up, frustration in the jerkiness of his movements. 'No. I've already told you, I'll consider your proposal with the others I receive. I don't want to discuss Evie's wedding now.'

'Why not? Let me show you what I'm thinking. I know—'

'You know nothing.' The words were loud, reverberating around the room. He closed his eyes and shook his head slowly from side to side, as if to clear their effect. When he looked at her, it was with a plea on his features. 'Just drop it, okay?'

No. It wasn't okay! She needed this! She needed

him to listen to her, to be sold on the wedding. The idea of going back to her life in England, watching her stepmother destroy her father's legacy, year on year, was anathema. Lucinda had set out for the Alps with one goal in mind and she intended to achieve it. For her father, and for herself. She needed to pick up this client—her future and freedom depended on it.

'Why won't you even talk about it?'

'I do not want strangers at the *castile*. This is my home. Mine. I will not share it.' Again, his voice was raised, and Lucinda felt the colour fade from her cheeks. He made a noise, a throaty growl, pacing from where he stood towards her.

He was so much bigger, but despite his obvious irritation, she wasn't afraid. Not even a little bit. The closer he got, the more her temperature spiked, the more aware she became of a thousand and one tiny details, like the stubble on his jaw and the groove to the side of his mouth, that formed a sort of dimple there. If he smiled, truly smiled, she imagined the effect would be quite breathtaking.

'It's your sister's too, isn't it?'

He was close enough that they were toe to toe. Lucinda argued with him for two reasons. She wanted to make a point and win it, but, more than that, she desperately wanted to argue, for the sake of it.

'Who the hell are you to come here and start

interfering in my life?' he demanded. Rightly, she had to admit. What did she think she was doing? This wasn't at all like Lucinda. None of this was her business. Wanting the job didn't give her a right to speak to him like this, nor to judge him for his decisions.

Arguing was one thing, but Lucinda felt the high ground slipping away from her. 'My proposal—'

'I don't give a damn about your proposal!' he ground out. 'You think you've done your research? Maybe you have. But not on me. You don't know anything about me, or you'd understand that hosting my sister's wedding at Castile di Neve is never going to happen. Not ever.' He drew in a deep breath, visibly attempting to defuse his anger. 'Now, if you were to come back to me with a different proposal, with the wedding at a hotel or restaurant, or at a hired castle in the south of France, or the whole goddamned South of France, for all I care, then I would consider it.'

'But what if this is what she wants?'

'You don't know her.'

'But you do,' she insisted quietly. 'Which do you think she'd prefer?'

He pressed his lips together, regarding her for several long, charged seconds. His eyes were like black lagoons, so dark and deep she almost felt as though she could dive into them.

'It's not going to happen.'

'But—'

'Submit something else,' he ground out, lifting a hand between them, as if to placate her or reassure her. But then, his hand moved, falling to her shoulder and staying there. His eyes dropped, studying his fingers, moving them slowly and frowning, as if he couldn't quite believe that he was touching her. She held her breath, wanting more, but too gun-shy to show that. After all, he'd already rejected her: twice. 'Anything else.' The words rumbled out of his chest, wrapping around her, all gravelled and hoarse.

But Lucinda didn't want to come up with just any proposal. She wanted to nail this. And yet…a job was a job, and this job had the potential to change her life. She bit down on her lower lip, her eyes latched imploringly to his. She could work something else out. She was great at events. She'd grown up living and breathing this sort of thing. Okay, her next proposal wouldn't be as perfect as this, but it would still be better than anyone else's. She just had to go back to the drawing board.

'Okay,' she agreed softly, nodding slowly.

He expelled a slow breath, relief obvious on his features. His hand stayed where it was and a thousand little darts danced through her bloodstream, radiating from her shoulder to her limbs and pooling in her abdomen. Warm heat flooded her nervous system and, without her consent, her body swayed forward, her breasts brushing his chest.

His only reaction was a soft groan, just low enough for her to catch.

'But I don't want to send it via email,' she said quietly, finding it difficult to speak. 'Let me present it to you in person.'

'No.' The denial was immediate and fierce.

'Why not?' She tilted her face up to his, her eyes sparking with his, her lips parted expectantly.

'Because I don't want to see you again.' And yet, in direct contradiction of that sentiment, his lips brushed hers, so lightly it was almost as if she'd imagined it. Her stomach knotted tightly, and she went to pull away, but the hand on her shoulder tightened, and his other wrapped around her back, drawing her to him. This time, when he kissed her, it wasn't soft or light, it was demanding and desperate, the same kind of desperation that had been rolling through her since the first moment they'd met.

When they'd kissed before, she'd seen stars, but there'd been an element of caution within Thirio, as though he were holding back. She felt none of that now. It was, if anything, quite the opposite. His total surrender to their passion was obvious.

He swore into her mouth, lifting her easily, wrapping her legs around his waist as he carried her into the lounge room, kissing her as his hands fondled her bottom. She groaned softly, pleasure spreading through her at the madness of this. Somewhere in the back of her mind, the Lucinda she ordinarily was, the woman who would *never* behave like this, was screaming at her to stop being so careless and impulsive. But, heck, impulsive felt so good, how could she resist? He laid her on the sofa, his body over hers, his strength and weight sublime.

'Why did you come here?' It was a rhetorical question, asked as he pulled away, his fingers finding the hem of the sweater she wore and pushing it up, revealing her flat stomach as his fingers grazed her flesh. Goosebumps lifted, covering her skin, his touch like silk, torture for how light it was, and how much more she wanted. When he grazed the fabric of her bra she arched her back and a low whimpering sound formed in the base of her throat. Pleasure sparked like fireworks, just beneath her skin.

'I shouldn't—' he muttered, lifting the sweatshirt over her head and tossing it onto the floor beside them. He didn't finish the sentence. Instead, he straightened, staring down at her, the look on his face impossible to interpret.

She didn't know what he was waiting for, but she knew that she wanted him, come what may.

'Yes, you should.' She sat up and dragged him down on top of her, kissing him with her soul's desire, tongues lashing, hands roaming, feeling his back through the softness of his shirt. When she reached beneath it, to lift it off him, as he had done to her, he flinched, and pulled it back down with one hand, his kiss growing more desperate, more urgent. She moved her hands lower, curling them into the waistband of his underpants, curving around his buttocks and pinning him close to her.

She had never wanted anyone, or anything, more than she wanted Thirio in that moment.

'I'm not going to have sex with you,' he said darkly, almost as though he were speaking to himself. The words acted like a whip on her spine. She froze, shifting a little so she could see his face, then moved again, feeling the hardness of his arousal between her legs. Of their own accord, her hips lifted silently inviting him, contradicting him. His eyes closed, but when he blinked open, there was fierce determination in his gaze.

'I can't.'

He dropped his mouth to hers, then moved it lower, dragging his lips over her chin to her décolletage, flicking the sensitive flesh there so she whimpered. But that was nothing to the sensations she felt when he lifted one of her breasts from the silk bra, brushing a nipple with his thumb, so millions of sparks flooded her system.

'Thirio,' she groaned, still stuck on his insistence that he wasn't going to have sex with her. Until he'd verbalised that, she hadn't realised that was what they'd been building to. Not just from their first kiss, but from the moment their eyes had met and something had lodged deep in her gut. Desire of the most soul-changing type. For the first time in Lucinda's life, she wanted something for herself and was reaching out to take it. The idea of being denied stuck in her throat like a bone.

His mouth moved to her other breast and through the soft fabric of her bra he took it in his mouth, pressing his teeth to the outline of her nipple with just enough pressure to make her pulse throb hard and heavy in her body.

'Thirio.' God, she loved his name. She loved the way it sounded, the way it felt. She loved the way he reacted when she said it. She loved the way his mouth felt on her breast, the way his arousal pushed against the cotton of her underpants. When he moved his mouth lower, kissing her stomach, her breath became light and rasping, and when he lowered the elastic of her knickers, she almost laughed, a soft, throaty sound of disbelief and desire, choked from her throat. But when his mouth teased her sex, she didn't laugh. She couldn't. Flames leaped through her, made all the more urgent when his tongue flicked her clitoris, sending shock waves through her.

Never before had she been kissed there, in her most sensitive place. His mouth was magic, pushing away any doubts she might have, tormenting her, pleasing her, making her see stars.

Her fingers drove through his hair, clinging on as if for dear life, and then, she was arching her back as tension grew, spinning through her, until she couldn't handle it any longer and she exploded in a flash of blinding light, white hot and incendiary. He held her hips still as the waves rolled through her, moving his mouth back to her breast and flicking it lazily with his tongue, then pushing up onto his hands to watch her, to stare at her, as pleasure flushed her face and her eyes took on a fevered sheen.

Desire was weakening her and making her feel like a goddess all at once.

'Thirio...' This time, his name was a husky request, heavy with need. She lifted a hand to his chest, feeling the steady tattoo of his beating heart through the cotton fabric of his shirt. 'I want—'

His lips pressed together and slowly he shook his head.

She didn't understand. Was he really saying 'no', to more of this? She could feel how badly he wanted her; she knew she wasn't imagining his desire.

'I can't.'

Not 'I don't want to'. But *I can't*.

She frowned, her fog of desire making thought almost impossible. 'Why not?'

But he was pulling away from her, standing, his arousal pushing against the cotton of his pants, making it impossible to ignore.

She looked from his erection to his face, her lips

parted, the loss of his physical proximity almost sucking the oxygen from her lungs.

'When you're ready, I'll fly you into town.'

Something inside her was spinning like a top, fast and out of control. A sense of helplessness gripped her. He was talking about sending her away. After what they'd just done. Or hadn't done. After what they'd just *started*, she amended, because the pleasure was building inside her even when he seemed to want to end their nearness.

Did he regret kissing her? Did he regret making her come? She sat up, straightening her bra, so her breasts were covered, her eyes probing his, trying desperately to understand.

'I have my car. I can drive.'

'The roads will still be icy.'

Then I can wait. The words died inside her. She stared at him, trying to comprehend, without wanting to ask the questions that were forming in her mind.

'Look.' He shook his head. 'That shouldn't have happened.'

She frowned. 'You didn't enjoy it.'

'That's a separate consideration.'

But he hadn't enjoyed it. Not as she had, and that knowledge brought a flush to her cheeks.

'I'll return your car when the roads clear.'

'Wait a second.' She lifted a hand to her forehead, trying to focus. 'I'm still on the "that shouldn't have happened" portion of the conversation. The car is kind of beside the point right now.'

His eyes bored into hers, but they were no longer fierce and cold, so much as almost…imploring. Her heart twisted sharply in her chest. 'I'm not in the habit of seducing beautiful, innocent strangers who seek shelter in my home.' A muscle throbbed in the base of his jaw.

'Are you worried you took advantage of me?' She raked his face with her eyes. 'Because you didn't. I mean… I definitely wanted that.'

'I know.' The gruff agreement didn't embarrass her as it could have. 'But I should have known better.'

'Why is what we did such a big deal?'

'You don't think sex is a big deal?' His cynicism was back, along with a healthy dose of mockery.

'We didn't have sex,' she pointed out.

'No, but we would have, if I didn't stop.'

'Yes,' she agreed quickly. There was no sense in lying.

'And that would be okay with you?' he pushed, his body language giving nothing away.

'Did you hear me asking you to stop?'

'*You're* in the habit of having sex with strangers?'

She frowned. She wasn't, but didn't particularly feel like having that conversation. 'You sound mighty judgmental for a guy who spent the better part of his early twenties with a different woman every night.'

Thirio's eyes narrowed, and for a moment he was unspeaking. But not silent. His eyes, his lips, the tension in his face, spoke volumes. She stood perfectly still, watching and waiting to see how he would respond.

'I'm not that person any more.' The words emerged darkly, each syllable clipped.

She tilted her head to the side. Something had happened to change him, and you didn't have to be a genius to guess what.

'Okay.' She nodded slowly. He clearly didn't want to talk about the fire, and she wasn't going to pry. But as for what had just happened between them? Well, it seemed only reasonable that they give it a bit more airtime. 'You're not. And nor am I, truth be told. That is to say, I don't seduce potential clients I happen to be stranded with no matter how hot they are.' His lips flickered a little, involuntarily, at her mention of 'hot'. 'Never. Not ever. But clearly there's something between us and I think we'd be stupid to ignore that.'

He didn't react. 'What do you have in mind?'

She frowned. A relationship? No. That wasn't what Lucinda wanted. And not with someone like Thirio. Right now, nothing mattered more to Lucinda than getting her father's company back in her name and returning it to its former prestige. Her dad deserved that, and Lucinda intended to deliver. A relationship would derail her from her goals. Besides, nothing about this man screamed 'happily ever after'.

'I don't have anything in mind,' she said after a beat. 'I just don't think you should act like we did something wrong.' For reasons she couldn't fathom, Lucinda didn't like the way he was sweeping it under the carpet.

'Fine.'

But his concession was meaningless. He was just trying to get rid of her. Anger bubbled inside Lucinda. How could he just brush her off like that?

Because it meant nothing to him.

And did it mean something to you?

She frowned, truly stumped by that question. Answers weren't within her grasp. She toyed with her necklace, staring at him, searching for something to say.

But he was withdrawing from her, his face a mask of disinterest.

'I'm not looking for a marriage proposal,' she said after a beat. 'But I enjoyed what we shared. I enjoyed kissing you and touching you, and I would have enjoyed getting to know you better. I would have enjoyed—' Heat flushed her cheeks. She shrugged, too shy to complete the sentence.

A muscle throbbed low in his jaw, making her wonder if he was grinding his teeth. Emotions emanated from him in waves, even when his body language was carefully controlled.

Silence beat between them, laced with tension. Lucinda could hear the throbbing of blood in her veins, washing through her ears, and she waited, but he said nothing for such a long time, she began to wonder if he didn't intend to speak. She took a step backwards, reconciling herself to that, when finally, his voice thickened the air between them.

'It shouldn't have happened.'

She opened her mouth to argue, but what was the point? Hadn't she learned how impossible it was to change someone's mind about you? Hadn't she learned the impossibility of getting someone to like you, love you, care for you, or even notice you? Her stepmother had given her a crash course in rejection, and Lucinda heeded those warnings now.

'Okay.' She shrugged as though his words didn't cut her to the quick. 'I'll get my things.'

She turned and walked away, head high, ignoring the strange sinking feeling in her stomach. He wasn't the first person to make her feel like crap, and he wouldn't be the last. But after the euphoric pleasure he'd given a moment earlier, the contrast stung.

CHAPTER SIX

THREE DAYS AFTER she left, he finally looked at it.

The goddamned plan. The wedding proposal she'd been so proud of.

It had sat in the centre of his kitchen counter since she'd handed it to him, and he'd wilfully, determinedly given it a wide berth, alternating between fury that she'd dare suggest he throw open his doors to a legion of strangers and an oversized sense of curiosity. She'd been so sure that her plan was worth the effort—the effort of coming to him, of waiting in his home, of getting stranded as a storm approached, of going toe to toe with Thirio, who no one ever dared argue with.

It was his curiosity that won out. Cracking the top off a beer, he regarded the document with a grim expression for several seconds before reaching for it and turning the cover page, slowly.

The first thing he noticed was her voice. Every word he read, he could hear in his head, as though she were speaking to him.

The next thing he noticed was the layout of

the document. He employed tens of thousands of people worldwide and he knew what went into creating professional, easy-to-understand reporting. Lucinda had nailed this. There was a lot of organisation, costing, and alternatives to cater for different contingencies. She'd said she was an administrative assistant at the company, but this plan was by far the most professional he'd seen. If she'd put this together on her own, then it was clear she had a fair idea what she was doing.

The last thing that struck Thirio, as he neared the end of the document, was how right she'd been.

Evie would love this wedding. It would be, as Lucinda had said, her dream come true.

He drained his beer, eyes focused on the piercingly blue sky beyond the kitchen.

His actions had taken a mother and a father from Evie, and then he'd taken himself away too. He'd spent the last six years hiding out in a castle on top of the world, in self-enforced purgatory. Somehow, she'd grown into a beautiful, intelligent, happy young woman, who'd fallen in love with a guy who worshipped her.

And Thirio had the power to make all her dreams come true.

To give her the kind of wedding she would adore, at the castle that had always meant so much to their family.

He just had to get over his own issues and agree

to make it happen. For Evie, he had to do that—she deserved nothing less.

'There's some ridiculously gorgeous guy waiting for you downstairs.'

Lucinda looked up from the filing cabinet at the sound of her stepsister's pronouncement. 'Who is it?'

'Beats me. I'm happy to interrogate him further, though.' Carina mimed fanning herself.

Lucinda frowned across at her stepsister. She was half tempted to agree. After all, the mountain of work that had built up while she was in Switzerland hadn't abated. Lucinda had been working even longer hours than usual to keep on top of it. Of course, that was an almost impossible task, given no one else in the business lifted a finger to take care of their own administrative work.

Why bother when Lucinda was there to clean it up?

She jerked the filing drawer closed with a clunk. The equipment needed upgrading. It all did. But her stepmother ploughed whatever profits the company made into funding her lavish lifestyle, rather than reinvesting in infrastructure or staff training. The company was stalling, and if Lucinda didn't act soon, all her father's work would be for nothing.

She spun around, skimming her eyes over Carina. Of the two stepsisters, she preferred Carina. She wasn't as interested in her appearance as Sofia, which was to say, she wasn't nearly as vain. She also made a point of being halfway decent to Lucinda, when Sofia and Elodie weren't around at least. And she had the added advantage of having never stolen Lucinda's boyfriend, unlike Sofia.

'That's okay,' Lucinda said with a tight smile. 'I'm due for a break anyway.' Besides, she was curious about the man asking for her.

As was Carina, apparently, because she walked behind Lucinda, down the stairs, so close she felt like a shadow.

Lucinda pulled the door to the reception area inwards, her caramel eyes scanning the space before landing on the very last person she'd ever expected to see again. Her gasp was involuntary. So too the flippy-flopping sensation in the pit of her stomach. He stood at the sound, their eyes locking and the air around them instantly sparking. It fired in Lucinda's veins too, and the whole world seemed to tip on its axis. She wasn't conscious of Carina, or the receptionist, or the sound of traffic whirring past the office.

There was only Thirio Skartos, his face, his body, the expensive suit that reminded her of the first day they'd met, his intense gaze, and memories of the way he'd touched her.

'Hello.' The words emerged soft and hoarse.

She cleared her throat; he didn't look away. Her insides tightened.

'Lucinda.' Hearing her name from his lips flushed her skin with goosebumps. Her eyes flared and all she could do was stare.

His gaze shifted beyond her shoulder, his lips compressing with obvious disapproval before his attention returned to her.

'Is there somewhere private we can talk?'

Her heart skipped so many beats she wondered if it was going to give out altogether.

'Um…' She hesitated, merely because this turn of events was so completely unexpected. He lifted one thick, dark brow, his expression otherwise unmoving. But that was enough to jolt her out of her state of surprise. 'Of course,' she said with a quick nod of her head. She turned around, almost bumping into Carina.

Lucinda read the question in her stepsister's eyes, but pretended not to. She didn't want to introduce Thirio, and somehow she just knew that the reclusive man didn't want his name being passed around. Sure enough, as they left the front office, Lucinda heard the receptionist whisper, none too quietly, 'I don't know! He wouldn't tell me who he is.'

Lucinda's breath came in tight little spasms. She walked up the stairs, conscious of him behind her, at around the height of her bottom, conscious of his nearness, of the fact that if he reached out he could touch her waist, oh, so easily, conscious of how badly she wanted that.

'We can speak in here.' She pushed open the door to the filing room, ignoring the prickle of despair that ran down her spine as he regarded the space.

'You don't have an office?'

'Why would I?' she asked with a grimace, turning to face him slowly, because she needed that time to brace for this.

'Right. You're not an events planner.'

Something bristled inside Lucinda. 'Not technically.'

'No.' He was staring at her as though seeking answers, but rather than asking her any question specifically, he just continued to stare, until the tension knotting inside Lucinda became almost unbearable.

'So,' she said after what felt like hours. 'What can I do for you, Mr Skartos?'

That same dark brow lifted skyward. 'That's a little formal, isn't it?'

Given what we did. The unspoken words hovered in the air, making Evie's skin tingle. 'Fine, Thirio,' she brushed aside, her voice shaking only the slightest amount when she said his name. It still filled out her mouth in a way that made her nerve endings tremble. 'What can I do for you?'

'I came to talk about Evie's wedding.'

Lucinda's pulse ratcheted up a gear. 'I'm still

working on another proposal,' she said after a beat. 'But I can get it to you by the end of the week.'

'No.' The word sliced through the air, thick and heavy.

Lucinda's brows drew together. 'Don't tell me you came all this way to ask me not to submit anything? This can't be because of what happened in Switzerland?'

He looked at her thoughtfully for several seconds. 'It's not.'

'Then why can't I offer a proposal? I have other ideas that I think your sister will love.'

He crossed his arms over his chest, and Lucinda had the sense he was fighting a war within himself. 'I doubt it,' was all he said, finally.

'Then why did you come here?' Frustration bubbled over into anger as Evie stared at the prospect of failure. This wedding had been her ticket to a better life, and she wanted, so badly, to be able to gain the account and know that the fee would enable her to buy out her stepmother.

'You misunderstood me.'

He took two steps, which, with his long stride, carried him to the wall opposite, then turned his back on her, his head tilted towards the top of the dark filing cabinets.

'I read your proposal,' he said after a beat.

Lucinda's brain scattered. It was the last thing she'd expected him to say. She couldn't even recall having left it. 'Did you?' she managed, eventually.

'Yesterday.'

She waited, her heart in her throat. She knew what he thought of it. He hated the idea. The castle was private. Lucinda had been so carried away in creating the dream event for Evie that she hadn't even stopped to consider how invasive her plan would seem to Thirio. Realistically, it had been doomed to fail.

'I'm sorry—' she said.

At the exact time Thirio turned to face her, and muttered, 'It's perfect.'

So Lucinda almost didn't hear him, and then she questioned if she'd *mis*heard him, because there was no way the same guy who'd refused to listen beyond the suggestion of turning his castle into a wedding venue for a weekend was now describing her plan as 'perfect'.

'I'm sorry,' she said again, with a different intonation this time. 'Did you just say—?'

He dipped his head in silent acknowledgement.

'But you hated the idea,' she blurted out, concern drawing her brows together.

'I still do.' His expression changed, flickering with a sadness she couldn't understand. 'But Evie would love it, and I want her to have the wedding of her dreams.' He took a step closer. 'You've created that. Or you will, once I authorise it.'

Lucinda's heart stammered and her eyes filled with stardust. 'You're serious?' For the first time in a long time, she felt something like relief cresting through her. Was it possible that everything might actually turn out okay? Well, not okay, because her dad would still be gone and that was a pain with which she'd never cope, but at least by buying the business, she could start running it as he would want.

'Yes.' He sounded as though he were preparing to have his teeth pulled, though, and, despite what this meant to her, hesitation crept into Lucinda.

'Listen, Thirio.' She moved towards him, lifting a hand and pressing it to his chest. Electricity arced through the tiny room, and yet it didn't feel strange to touch him. Quite the opposite. The second her fingers connected with his chest, something locked in place inside Lucinda. 'I can come up with something else. I've learned a heap about your sister from the research I've done. I know I can pull together a dream wedding scenario that doesn't involve the Castile de Neve.'

He held her gaze and yet it was as though he was staring right through her, fixating on something else entirely. 'When Evie was a child, she was badly bullied at school.'

Lucinda's brows knitted together. 'I didn't know that.'

He spoke as though she hadn't. 'It was very cruel. She was much smaller than the other girls, and she struggled academically. It took several years for my parents to realise she had dyslexia. By then, she'd been made to feel as though she were stupid. I remember one Christmas, when we were at the *castile*, I discovered her crying in her room. She'd found a note that had been stuffed into her book by a so-called friend, saying some pretty ghastly things. Evie told me that the *castile* was the only place she felt like herself, the only place she felt safe from the cruelty of other children.'

Lucinda shook her head softly. 'That's awful.'

He nodded once.

'I took her into the forest and, together, we fashioned a sled. It took us two full days, and while we worked I asked her questions about the children who were being cruel, the sorts of things they were saying. At first, she was tight-lipped, but the more we worked, side by side, the more she shared, so I came to understand how devastating their treatment was. I hadn't noticed before. My sister had been putting on such a brave face— that's something she does, you know.'

Lucinda nodded gently. She didn't know why he was confiding this, but she liked listening to him, particularly when speaking about his life.

'I haven't always been there for her. In fact, I've been a pretty crappy older brother, most of the time. But on that one afternoon, when I watched her ride the sled we'd made down the mountain, I saw her face glow with happiness, I saw her laugh for the first time in a long time, and I remember thinking I would do anything to know she was happy like that, always. And I can do that again now.' His Adam's apple shifted visibly as he swallowed. 'I want her to have her dream wedding.'

'But I can—'

He lifted a finger, pressing it to her lips, the colour of his irises shifting at the contact. 'You have already come up with the perfect wedding. Well, almost.' His lips twisted in a rueful expression that was almost a grin.

'Almost?' Her own voice was hoarse, the word whispering around his finger, her warm breath spiralling between them.

'There are some changes, mainly to the logistics. Considerations of which you could not have been aware. I also have some suggestions for the accommodation. Again, you are not familiar with the castle as I am, and therefore couldn't have known how many rooms could be made available to guests.'

'I wasn't sure if you'd want—'

'It makes sense.' His expression gave little away. 'My parents used to host enormous balls there every year, before they…' His voice trailed into nothing, and sympathy tightened her lips into a small frown.

'I'd love to talk logistics with you,' she said after a pause, fully aware that he wouldn't want to be drawn further on the tragic loss of his parents. 'Do you have time now?'

'I have another meeting to get to,' he said

quickly. As if belatedly realising his finger was still pressed to Lucinda's lips, he dropped it quickly, his hand flexing by his side. 'What about tonight?'

Her heart stammered. 'Tonight?'

Something sparked between them. A silent understanding. A risk. A temptation. 'Purely business,' he assured her.

Only Lucinda wasn't assured. She felt thwarted. Every single cell in her body was reverberating with a need to kiss him, as strongly as ever. If not stronger, for the fact she hadn't seen him in days.

But she'd be crazy to push any kind of romantic agenda with him now. He was her saviour. This wedding was going to make all her dreams come true. Sure, she might desire him in a way that caused her heart to lurch and her pulse misfire, but she couldn't act on that. Not without potentially jeopardising this business arrangement.

Even as that occurred to her, she forced herself to grapple with an unappealing thought. 'Thirio, this isn't for any other reason, right?'

His frown was reflexive. 'Such as?'

Heat stained her flesh. 'Such as, what happened between us. This isn't some... I don't know...compensation for...'

'Do I need to compensate you?'

'No! That's exactly my point. As I said that

morning, what we did was very mutual. Actually, it wasn't, but you know what I mean.'

His smile surprised Lucinda. It was the work of an instant, a literal flash across his face before darkness and cynicism returned. 'No, Lucinda. I'm here because I took the time to read your proposal, as you rather passionately advocated for me to do. And I'm not sorry, because you were right. The details you've thought of were very impressive. I know Evie will love it.'

Lucinda had been certain of that, and yet as she heard it from Thirio pleasure swarmed through her, warming her, his praise a balm she'd not known before. Despite all the work she did to keep the company going, she was never commended for it. Seeing things run smoothly was the only reward—and it had been, until recently, almost enough.

'There's one thing I don't understand,' she said after a small pause.

'Yes?'

'How come she's asking you to organise this? I mean, it's clear that weddings aren't your forte, and most brides are ridiculously invested in the details. Why not Evie?'

He opened his mouth but said nothing, then shook his head, just once. 'We will discuss that tonight.'

A *frisson* of anticipation ran the length of her spine.

'Okay. Where? When?'

He named an exclusive hotel in central London. 'Eight o'clock?'

'Fine,' she said with a small nod. 'It's a date.'

CHAPTER SEVEN

BUT IT WASN'T a date, it was business, she reminded herself and the butterflies that had taken up residence in her stomach for the millionth time that night, as she walked through the revolving glass door of the swish hotel foyer. She was underdressed. Then again, how could she not be? Lucinda didn't own anything even remotely fancy enough for a place like this, so she'd relied on one of her favourite outfits—flattering black trousers and an oyster-colour silk blouse with a bow at the neck, teamed with black ballet slippers and her trusty briefcase: a leather document wallet that had belonged to her father. It was a good luck charm for Lucinda, and how she felt that she needed luck tonight!

Not to land the job. She was sure she had that in the bag. But to survive the next hour or so, discussing logistics with Thirio. She looked around the foyer, but couldn't see him. Frowning, she took a seat, knees trembling a little. She opened her briefcase, pulling out her proposal, skimming it, re-familiarising herself with the details. She'd also brought her secondary proposal, just in case he wanted to see that too. Now that he'd agreed to go with her plan A, she felt more than a hint of compunction at having talked him into this. He valued his privacy and she wasn't sure she was comfortable invading it any more.

'Miss Villeneuve?'

At the mention of her name, she looked up sharply, the smile on her face instinctive. Lucinda, though naturally beautiful, had been told for a great many years by her stepmother and stepsisters that she was plain and awkward, with unremarkable colouring and features, and their assessment of her had become a part of what she accepted as gospel. She therefore didn't notice the appraising glint in the man's eyes as he drew nearer, nor the appreciative smile that shaped his lips.

'Yes?'

'Mr Skartos will see you now.'

She blinked, wide caramel eyes flicking around the foyer. 'Will he? Because I can't see him.'

The man, aged somewhere in his forties with dark hair that greyed a little at the temples, smiled once more at her joke. 'He's in his suite. This way, please.'

'Oh.' She stood, darting the tip of her tongue out and moistening her lips nervously. The man led her to an elevator, and pressed the button to summon it.

'Do you work for Thirio?'

'Yes.'

That interested Lucinda, and for reasons that went well beyond the professional. 'What do you do?'

The man's expression showed bemusement. 'I'm his personal assistant. Or rather, I am where it concerns his UK business.'

'Does he have much business here?'

'Enough to keep me very, very busy,' the man promised with a wink as the lift arrived and they stepped into it. He swiped a card and the doors swooshed closed, the lift immediately beginning its ascent.

The answer gave little away. In fact, it only raised more questions in curious Lucinda, but they weren't questions she needed answers to. At least, not to be able to do her job. She needed to focus on the wedding, not all the little things she wanted to know about Thirio.

'I'm Lucinda,' she said as the lights indicated they were travelling higher and higher.

'Travis.' Did he know how nervous she was? The butterflies in her stomach wouldn't settle. She took a deep breath and exhaled slowly, trying to calm down. Was she nervous about the pitch and contracts? Was it adrenalin because of what this job would mean for her, personally and professionally? Or was it anticipation at seeing Thirio again, and this time in the privacy of his hotel suite? Definitely a combination, but mostly the latter.

The doors pinged open to a small carpeted foyer, with two doors coming off it. Travis led her to one, then knocked twice before pushing open the door, holding it wide to allow Lucinda to enter.

She knew the hotel to be exclusive, and everything about it had seemed quite grand, but, regardless of that, nothing had prepared her for what she'd find in this, the suite on the very top floor of the hotel. And she knew it was the top floor because of the skylights above the lounge area that would, in the morning, provide a delicious golden glow as the sun bathed Knightsbridge in gold. *Not* that she had any intention of still being here in the morning, of course!

'Enjoy your evening, Lucinda.'

Travis was already leaving, leaving her alone in this beautiful hotel living room.

She moved towards the lounge chairs on autopilot, running her fingers over the thickly stuffed arm of one, before taking several steps towards the floor-to-ceiling glass doors that opened out onto a small terrace. Just as she shifted her hand to the door to slide it open, Thirio did the same, from outside, so they stood, face to face, separated only by a piece of glass. Startled, Lucinda took several quicks s tep back, clutching her briefcase like a security blanket. It felt as though a frog had taken up residence inside her throat, her pulse was ticcing so fast and hard.

He opened the door and the sultry night air breathed in, wrapping around her, so she inhaled deeply.

'I've always loved this time of year,' she said, out of nowhere, then felt like an absolute idiot for saying the first thing that popped into her head.

Thirio, though, didn't look at her as though she'd said anything stupid. 'Why?'

'It reminds me of summer vacation.' She smiled, despite the tension radiating through her.

'Care to join me?' He gestured towards the balcony. She looked over his shoulder, nerves bursting through her.

'I won't bite,' he promised, after several beats of hesitation.

That's a shame. Her involuntary response almost brought a gasp to her mouth but she controlled the impulse—just. But the way his eyes held hers showed he'd heard her thoughts anyway, or perhaps had a similar thought himself.

Lucinda swallowed to clear the thickness in her throat as she stepped out onto the deck. It ran along the whole frontage of his suite, with thick white concrete railings and tumbles of geraniums spilling over the edges, coating the air in bursts of pink and red. Clumps of daisies sat in terracotta pots and there was a small plunge pool, illuminated by turquoise lights.

'Where did you go on summer vacations?'

Her hands squeezed the briefcase more tightly. 'As a girl, my father would take me to Cornwall every year. We stayed at the same little house. Nothing grand—close to a cove, covered in stucco with seashells pressed into every available surface. I used to dream that I was a mermaid,' she confessed with a soft laugh. 'I loved it there. The air smelled of salt and sunshine, and the night sky was so clear, you could see every star in the heavens.'

She tilted her face towards him, to find his eyes settled on her features in a way that made her stomach twist.

'What would you do on these vacations?'

'Nothing particularly special. At least, not to anyone else. It was just the little, everyday things. We'd get ice cream in the afternoon—two scoops for me—and walk until we'd finished it; my fingers would get all sticky. I remember the sound of seagulls hovering over the fishermen's boats, and the way fish would flip and flop in the nets. There was a black cat that belonged to the property, or lived there regardless of whether it belonged or not,' she tacked on wryly. 'Benedict.' The memory came back to her fully formed and immediate. 'He loved having the fur between his ears scratched. For dinner, we'd go to a little pub on the edge of the water: The Anchor and Grace. I'd get the same thing every night—fish with peas and gravy. I loved it.' Her smile was wistful. 'After losing my dad, all those memories took on a renewed significance.'

She didn't look at Thirio. She couldn't. She didn't trust herself not to give into the emotion that was tightening her throat, and the last thing she wanted to do was cry in front of him. If she had looked, she would have seen that he was frowning contemplatively, looking at the view of Knightsbridge, his handsome, symmetrical face silhouetted against the grey of the night sky and the darkness of Hyde Park.

'After I heard about Evie's wedding, I devoured every interview she'd done. I know that must sound creepy, but I wanted to be prepared, and weddings are so personal. From the first interview, I felt such an affinity with her and what she's been through. Or more specifically, what's missing in her life, because I feel that too.' Now, she turned to face Thirio, steeling herself against the emotional response that was softening her insides. His face remained tilted away, so she could only stare at his autocratic profile, the strength of his cheekbones, nose and brow quite remarkable. 'I feel it right here, you know?' She pressed her fingers between her breasts, staring up at him imploringly, not sure what she wanted him to say, only that it was suddenly vitally important that he understand.

Slowly, he turned to face her, the strength of his

chiselled features almost taking her breath away, because there was such beauty in his face, and such sadness in his eyes, that she ached to comfort him. Evie's loss was also Thirio's. Where Evie had spoken quite openly about the deaths of her parents, and how it had affected her, Thirio had been resolutely silent. There had been no interviews, and he had disappeared from that day onwards. But none of that was confirmation that he didn't carry the same burden of grief. If anything, it was confirmation that he felt just the same, only he didn't know how to express that intense loss.

Would he discuss it with her? Would he let down that wall, if she prompted him to do so? Or would he withdraw, and turn right back into the beastly, angry man he'd been that afternoon at the *castile*?

'I can't imagine how hard it's been, on both of you,' she said softly, gently, giving him every opportunity to step slowly away from the conversation, to lead her in a different direction.

'Can't you? It seems to me like you can imagine perfectly. Your father's death must have tilted your world off its axis, given how close you were.'

So he was going to deflect. 'I felt very alone.'

'And your stepmother?' he prompted, his eyes tunnelling into hers. She felt exposed and seen, and Lucinda didn't much like that.

'What about her?'

'Did she fill a role for you, after your father died?'

Died. Not a euphemism, like most people employed. *Passed away. After you lost him. Went away.* Thirio was direct and to the point. He knew this grief, he carried its heavy burden also, and so he spoke as one survivor to another.

'You could say that,' Lucinda prevaricated, not naturally given to badmouthing anyone. Life was too short to carry grudges—how many times had her father said that? It was for his sake she'd forgiven her stepmother on so many occasions, for his sake she'd turned a blind eye and just kept her head down, focusing on the work that needed to be done for the company to prosper.

'But not a good one,' he pushed.

'I suppose you could say that,' she admitted uncomfortably after a beat.

'Yet you don't want to say it.'

Her lips twisted in something between a grimace and a smile. It was strange how he understood her so completely. 'I don't know if anything's served by trashing my stepmother behind her back,' Lucinda conceded. 'Besides, I think she's done the best she could, given...'

'Given?' he prompted, when she snapped her lips shut, mid-sentence.

'Her...personality,' she finished without meeting his eyes.

'It just kills you to say something negative about someone, doesn't it?' There was surprise in his voice, and it drew her gaze right back to his face.

'Well, that's not entirely true,' she murmured softly. 'I seem to remember throwing some home truths at your feet when I was at your castle.'

His lips flattened. 'Nothing I didn't deserve.'

She angled her face upwards. 'Careful, Thirio. That's getting awfully close to an apology.'

His response was a short laugh, entirely lacking in humour. 'It's not.' But he brought his face closer to hers, their eyes remaining locked. 'Let's not forget, you were an unwanted houseguest.'

Unwanted. Just as she'd been all her life. The words were spoken with a hint of irony, so she couldn't tell if he was joking or not, but, either way, it didn't lessen the sting. It wasn't his fault, so much as almost a decade of conditioning. She cleared her throat, furrowing her brow as she tried to get a grip on things. 'Anyway, I came here to discuss the wedding, not my personal life.'

'And yet I find myself thinking a lot about your personal life,' he responded immediately, the words growled, his expression showing that he resented that.

'Oh.' She swallowed past her knotty throat. 'Do you?'

His nod was just one movement of his head.

'What sorts of things do you wonder about?'

'Are you single?'

She lifted both brows towards the heavens. 'Do you think I'd let what we did happen if I had a boyfriend?'

'I don't know anything about you,' he said slowly, each syllable spoken with care.

'You know some things.'

'Such as?'

'You know that I'm honest, remember?'

He nodded slowly, an intensity in his gaze that spread like wildfire through her belly.

'Also, you know that I can be pushy when something's important.'

His eyes seemed to spark with hers. 'And I know what you sound like when you are coming,' he added with a husk to his voice that made her pulse spin wildly.

'Thirio…' His name emerged as a gravelled admission—but of what?

'You are so beautiful.'

His words jolted her, because she knew they weren't the truth. 'You don't need to say that.'

His eyes narrowed, his thumb lifted, of its own accord, to her lower lip, rubbing across it, and his eyes hungrily chased the gesture, showing how badly he wished that it were his mouth in his finger's place. 'Why shouldn't I? It's the truth.'

Her eyes fluttered shut. True or not, his words were magical, weaving through her, so she tilted her head back slowly, just a little, swaying forward without intending to.

'I swore this wouldn't happen.'

She blinked, trying to focus on his face, but it

was too close, so close that there was only a hair's breadth between them. 'Why?'

The simplicity of the question didn't change the fact the answer was complex and knotty. He hesitated, his face so close, his breath fanning her cheek. 'Does it matter? Apparently, I have no intention of taking my own damned advice.'

Adrenalin pumped through her, filling her body with steel. But she held her ground, pulling away ever so slightly, even when every fibre of her being was drawing her closer, making her want him with unmatched desire. 'It matters to me. You pushed me away last time. I think I deserve to understand why.'

Her insistence seemed to connect with him, and he straightened, a muscle twisting at the base of his jaw, the subtle action catching her attention, so her eyes dropped to it on autopilot. 'Did I hurt your feelings?'

He asked the question without a hint of sarcasm. In fact, there was genuine concern in his eyes, something that slowed her heart almost to a stop. 'Yes,' she said honestly, tilting her chin defiantly. 'Like I said that morning, I wasn't looking for a marriage proposal, but you totally shut me down. It made me feel…' *Unwanted. Cast aside.* But to admit that was to reveal too much of herself, and so she simply shrugged. 'Immaterial,' she finished eventually.

He made a small sound, rich with disbelief. 'If

I thought you were "immaterial", I would have had sex with you.'

'What does that even mean?' she whispered.

'You're obviously sweet and kind and relatively inexperienced and I am not the kind of man who can be the Prince Charming you deserve.'

She furrowed her brow, even as his compliments ran through her like treacle. 'Who says I want Prince Charming?' She shook her head. 'Who says I even *believe* in such a thing?' After all, she'd learned the hard way that fairy tales were solidly the provenance of children and make-believe.

'Everything about you,' he ground out, but he moved closer again, putting a hand on her hip. It was nothing. The lightest touch, but it seared her skin and at the same time there was such sweet respectfulness to the contact, that her chest heaved with the weight of her heart's fullness.

'You're wrong.'

'About this?' His eyes dropped to her lips and her heart stammered; she wanted him to kiss her so fiercely it hurt.

Slowly, she shook her head, lower lip drawn between her teeth. 'Not about this.'

His eyes flared with an emotional response she couldn't understand. 'What is it about you?'

'I...what do you mean?'

'At no other time have I wanted—' He shook his head in exasperation. 'I shouldn't want—'

'But you do.'

He moved closer, his eyes glowing with intensity. 'I want things I promised myself I couldn't have. I want to make love to you, all night. I want to carry you over my shoulder, to my bed, to drop you down and pleasure you until you can hardly think, let alone speak. I want to taste you again, and feel your body tremble against my mouth.'

Lucinda closed her eyes, tilting her head back at the sensual imagery he was evoking. 'But what I want most of all is to resist this, even when desire is almost crippling me.'

It was the last thing she expected him to say. Her eyes flickered open. 'Why?'

One word, uncertain and confused, hovered in the balmy evening air between them.

'What do you want?' he responded, lifting his thumb to her lips and dragging it across the pillowy flesh there.

Lucinda drew in a sharp breath to quell her chaotic nerves. But for Lucinda, who'd been focused on one goal for so many years, and had barely allowed herself to have dreams or hopes of a personal nature, she struggled to verbalise her needs. Was it fear of rejection? That definitely played a part. But it was also just a lack of experience with going after what—or who—she wanted. Yet this was no ordinary situation, and Thirio Skartos no ordinary man. This demanded that she push herself outside her comfort zone, and find words for the desires that were causing the rapid spasming of her heart.

'Everything you've just said you want, I want too.'

CHAPTER EIGHT

HIS EYES CLOSED on her husky admission. 'And then what?'

'And then,' she said with a thoughtful frown, 'we plan the wedding.' His eyes sprang open and heat stole into Lucinda's cheeks. 'Evie and Prince Erik's,' she clarified. 'Obviously.'

'Yes,' he said, but still didn't move to kiss her. Frustration and impatience leaped through Lucinda, making her fingertips tingle. 'And after that?'

She narrowed her eyes. 'I've told you, I'm not looking for anything more. I don't believe in fairy-tale happy endings.'

'And yet you've planned a wedding that belongs in a Disney film.'

'Because it's what your sister wants,' she said after a small pause.

'And you?'

'Marriage is nowhere on my horizon,' she insisted. Nor, she wanted to add, was love. The idea of opening herself up to another person made her break out in a fine sweat. How could she ever allow herself to love and hope to be loved back? 'Until I met you, I didn't think any kind of relationship was,' she said with sincerity.

'Why not?'

She shook her head slightly. 'That's not important.'

'Isn't it?' He seemed to stare into her soul. She wanted to box away her feelings and hide from him. This was a part of her she didn't want to show!

'Perhaps it's better to say it's not relevant,' she murmured after a beat. 'Suffice it to say, what we both admitted we feel a moment ago is the beginning and end of this for me.' She forced herself to be bold and say it, to really strip things back to basics. 'Sex,' she rushed out, her cheeks flushing pink. 'And nothing more.'

'You really think you can operate that way?'

'Of course.' She jutted her chin out with determination.

He studied her for a very long time, but she held her ground, refusing to move away, or to admit that she'd never had a no-strings relationship. Refusing to admit that, in fact, she'd only ever had one boyfriend and that had ended spectacularly badly, when she'd walked in to find him in bed with her stepsister Sofia.

Oh, she wanted Thirio. And she would do almost anything to have him. The needs that were spinning inside her were no longer human, able to be contained by thought and will; they were so much bigger.

She'd been waiting for him to kiss her, needing him to do so with every cell of her body, and yet, it was only when their bodies connected that she remembered she had the power too. She could kiss him! Pushing up onto the tips of her toes, she didn't hesitate for even a moment before pressing her lips to his, moaning softly as they parted under her ministrations. He was very still at first but then, slowly, his hand came around her back, holding her to him, and he began to kiss her back, a guttural noise of his own thickening in his throat before bursting into her mouth. She felt it roar through her soul.

His tongue flashed into her mouth once, and then again, duelling with hers, dominating her as he had done in the kitchen of the castle. She pushed up higher, delighting in this feeling, relishing the prospect of what was to come, even as her body felt almost tormented by the strength of this desire. Her hands lifted, linking behind his neck, so her breasts were crushed to his chest and she was conscious of every single detail in that moment. Her nipples tingled against the fabric of her bra, the skin on her arms lifted with goosebumps and his breath mingled with hers, warm and frantic.

He swore—at least, she thought he did—in another language, Greek, perhaps, then moved, stepping forward and propelling her with him, away from the terrace railings, towards the wall of the penthouse suite. Her back collided with the cold stone and his mouth took hers again, so hot in contrast. His hands lifted the silk fabric of her blouse, separating it from her trousers, so his fingertips could brush her bare skin, running over her flat stomach with a sense of possession that was startling for how right it felt. Then again, it had been like this at the castle as well.

His hands roamed higher, his kiss grew deeper, but when he cupped her breasts she broke away, gasping loudly, because the sensation was so good that heat and moisture pooled between her legs, and suddenly, her impatience was almost ready to burst the banks of any kind of self-control she was trying to hold onto.

'Please, Thirio,' she moaned, pulling at the ribbon of her blouse and loosening the top button. He dropped his mouth to the flesh below her earlobe, his stubble grazing her sensitive skin there as he finished unbuttoning her blouse then removed it completely. His hands moved to her bra straps next, pushing them down her arms, then reaching between her back and the wall to unfasten the clip with impressive efficiency. The bra fell away, and she shivered at the sensation of the night air on her naked breasts.

He kissed his way south, dragging his mouth

from the base of her neck to the top of one of her breasts, kissing the flesh there before moving lower, claiming a nipple, drawing it into his mouth and sucking on it then rolling it with his tongue, while a hand cupped her other breast and held her close.

She lifted a leg, wrapping it around his, drawing him closer, so his arousal was hard and strong against her womanhood. Lucinda had barely any experience with men. One boyfriend, what felt like eons ago, and some very unsatisfying attempts at making love—a first for both of them. But somehow, her body knew what she needed to do, and that was to try everything possible to be *closer* to him. They were welded together, and yet it wasn't enough. All she could think was that she needed *more*.

'Please,' she groaned, incandescent with desire. 'I want you.'

But suddenly, the magic stopped. His mouth pulled away from her breast; his head lifted and he stared at her as though only just seeing her for the first time. There was such confusion in the depths of his eyes that desire waned, making space for concern.

But, oh, she didn't want him to stop! She needed him—this—to keep going! 'Thirio, it's okay.' She didn't know why, but she sensed he needed reassurance. 'I want this to happen.'

'I know that.' The words rumbled out of his

chest, as though dragged up from the depths of his soul. 'But I don't.'

She flinched, the denial stinging. Except she *knew* he wanted her. The proof of that was still pressed against her. 'Why are you fighting this?'

His eyes closed and he drew in a deep breath, as though trying to control his desire, to fight this—her—just as she'd said. Sure enough, when he opened them, there was clarity and determination in his features. He stepped back then crouched down, lifting her bra from the ground. Slowly, he began to slide the straps over her arms.

Lucinda stood there, letting him do that, but when he went to reach behind her and clasp the bra in place, she took advantage of his closeness and angled her face, kissing the base of his jaw, flicking the flesh there with her tongue. She felt his harsh intake of air.

'Lucinda.' Her name was both a command and a desperate, agonising plea. 'Stop.'

She could stand strong in the face of some rejection, but not much, and the strength of that word had her withdrawing immediately. Not just physically, but with all of herself.

'Why?' A plaintive whisper. She needed to understand—she deserved that, didn't she? 'I'm not made of glass. You won't break me.'

'No,' he agreed, lifting a hand and cupping her face, the kindness of the gesture somehow hateful. 'But I'll be breaking something else. Something important to me.'

'What? A vow of celibacy or something?' she joked, the words infused with angry spite.

But he tilted his face away, looking towards the lights dancing in the distance. 'Something like that.'

Her lips parted, confusion swamping her. 'But—are you serious?'

He looked down at her, his lips a grim line on his face. Mockery tinged his expression. 'Unfortunately, yes. And it means more to me than I can explain.' He stepped backwards, pulling away from her in every way now. 'Come inside when you're ready. We will discuss the wedding.'

Desire was not so easy to tame. She wished, more than anything, that she could simply switch off her feelings and focus on the plans she'd come to discuss. But where Thirio was completely himself again, looking as focused and calm as ever, Lucinda's nerves were still skittling around inside her, so she had to clasp her hands behind her back to stop them from visibly shaking.

'We will need more security than you've allowed for.' He turned the page, running the pen through the section pertaining to guest protection. 'Nalvania will send a contingent of guards for the royal family, but the other guests are also high profile. I will station checkpoints here—' he marked a cross on the aerial photograph she'd included in her proposal '—here and here, as well as drones in the valley, and obviously at all the entrances.'

'Are you really worried that the guests will be… attacked? It's a wedding,' she pointed out, shivering a little at the need for such defence.

'I am worried about press intrusions, primarily,' he said with a lift of his shoulders. 'But yes, there is also the concern of kidnapping.'

'Kidnapping!' she repeated, aghast.

'It never hurts to play it safe.'

Was that why he'd backed away from her? Was it some kind of safety concern? But she'd told him she wasn't made of glass. No, it had to be this vow of celibacy.

Unless that was just a particularly heavy-handed way to put her off. After all, it was almost impossible to imagine a man as virile as Thirio Skartos avoiding sex. And since when? She'd seen enough evidence of his hectic love life on the Internet.

But the accident. The fire. Her eyes lifted to his face, appraisingly, and her heart skidded to a stop. Was it possible that beneath this big, strong billionaire there was the broken heart of a young man who'd buried both his parents? She knew that he'd hidden himself away in the castle ever since, but had he locked himself away in every possible way, too?

'My sister is hopeful of keeping the guest list small. At this stage, she has said there will be around one hundred and fifty people in attendance. The ballroom can more than cope with this number.'

'I was hoping you'd say that,' she replied, her voice hoarse, and concentration scattered.

'Did you see it, when you were at the castle?'

She shook her head slowly. 'No.'

'Not when you were waiting for me to return?'

Her cheeks flushed pink. 'No. Contrary to what you might have imagined, I didn't go prowling through your private space. I came inside because my car was freezing and no one was answering the door.'

'Did it occur to you that I might not return home that night at all?'

She frowned. 'No, actually. It didn't. I think I was just so intent on presenting my plan to you that I didn't think about anything else.'

'Why did it matter so much to you?' He placed the pen down on the tabletop, stretching back in his chair and fixing her with a level stare. She wished she could channel some of his casual attitude, but she could still feel the ghost of his touch on her body, his kisses, and both memories were weakening her. 'It can't be just that you wanted to help out a fellow orphan.'

His perceptiveness no longer surprised her. 'When I read about your sister's engagement, and your parents' tragic deaths, I wanted to do what I could to give her the perfect, perfect wedding. That was my first thought. But...' She hesitated, wondering if the admission she was about to make would lessen her in some way. Nonetheless, she felt compelled to be completely upfront with him. 'I did have a more personal motive, as well.'

Silence crackled around them, and he waited for several beats before lifting a single dark brow and prompting, 'Which was?'

She sipped her water to buy time, then chose her words carefully. 'For years I have helped my stepmother and stepsisters from behind the scenes. I've dotted the i's and crossed the t's to make sure our events went off smoothly. When there were problems, I smoothed them over with our clients. But I have never had my own event to manage.' She toyed with her necklace thoughtfully. 'Frankly, I want the fee from this, all for myself.'

His surprise was evident.

'I know that must sound mercenary,' she said with a grimace. 'But it's very important to me. I need this fee, Thirio, and the acclaim the wedding will bring to me.'

'You speak like someone who intends to go out on her own. Are you opening your own company?'

'No,' she denied quickly. 'Not exactly.'

'Then what?'

She had hoped to avoid getting into too many details, but again, sitting opposite Thirio, the truth seemed to bubble out of her, almost without her awareness. 'My father died a year after they were married. He loved my stepmother very much and I think—I hope—she loved him. But I know now that before going through with the wedding, she insisted on a prenuptial agreement. It's ironclad. And my father paid very little attention to the terms. After all, he had no intention of divorcing her. She was very specific though about how his will should be updated.' Lucinda's voice cracked a little. 'So they married, and he got his affairs in order as required, with no thought that it would ever come to matter.'

'What were the terms of the will?'

'That everything would pass to her.' Lucinda's voice was blanked of emotion, but she felt it heavy in her heart. 'Our family home, my father's business—that I had spent all my spare time at growing up, because there was no one to look after me—and all his savings. I have nothing, Thirio. Everything became hers. I depended on her "generosity" after his death. I have ever since.'

Silence cloaked them as he digested this. 'And so this fee will enable you to start your own life,' he said, the words strangely thick.

She shook her head. 'I don't want my own life. I want the life I should have had. That business should be mine. My stepmother is only interested in using the database to find rich husbands for Sofia and Carina. She likes the income, and the cachet, but I believe she'd sell it to me—for the right price.'

'This fee surely wouldn't be enough.'

'No,' she agreed with a small nod. 'But it's a deposit. I've spoken to a couple of banks and I believe I'll be able to secure a loan.' There was doubt there, but she couldn't allow it to infiltrate her mind. She was living on hopes, and she had to hold onto them, or she might fall apart. 'It's all I've wanted, Thirio. For years. I decided so long ago that I would make this right. And then every time she—'

'Go on,' he urged, voice gravelled, when she stopped, mid-sentence.

Lucinda hesitated, running a finger around the rim of her water glass. 'Every time she was unkind to me, or mismanaged the company, or said something unfavourable about my father, I'd just hold onto the idea that, soon, I would fix it. That I would erase her from his business and my life.' She scrunched up her face. 'I know that must make me seem like a terrible person. She's my stepmother, after all.'

Thirio's stare was so intense it was almost unnerving. 'In what ways has she been unkind to you?' he asked, after several long seconds had stretched between them.

Lucinda's stomach looped.

So. Many. Ways.

She zipped her lips closed before the telling response could emerge, dropping her eyes to the table.

'What happened to honesty?' Thirio prompted. And though the words were soft, they had the cut-through of a sharp metal blade. She flinched a little, her eyes flittering to his before she could stop them.

'I—' She darted her tongue out, licking her lower lip. His eyes traced the gesture and her heart stammered. He had a point. An hour ago, she'd been wanting to sleep with Thirio, and yet she balked at revealing this information to him? It wasn't a secret. Her stepmother had eviscerated her publicly and openly, shouting at Lucinda in shopping malls and in front of staff at the office. 'I suppose you could say she never liked me very much,' Lucinda whispered. 'She hadn't really known my father all that long, then he died, and she was saddled with an extra child.'

He frowned. 'Were you difficult?'

'I was fifteen and in grief, so possibly.'

His eyes narrowed thoughtfully. 'Somehow, I doubt that.'

She flicked her glance back to the tabletop, running her finger over a knot in the timber surface. 'Me too.' She bit into her lip. 'I don't know why she hates me.' Lucinda shook her head, then squared her shoulders. 'But she does, and I've finally learned to stop trying to fix that. She'll never like me.'

'So why not walk away? Why does the business matter so much to you?'

'Because it was his,' she said immediately. 'I basically grew up there. As a little girl, I used to send faxes and open the mail. As I got older, I began to type letters and schedule bookings. By the time he passed away, I was already known to most of his clients and venues. The company's in my blood, and seeing the way she's running it into the ground makes me want to... I don't know... throw something at a wall!' She finished with an exasperated growl, then tried to bring herself back under control. 'I'm really good at this, Thirio.'

'I can see that.' He thumbed through the plan absent-mindedly. 'Your proposal is comprehensive and creative. I was very impressed when I read it.'

And despite having, only moments earlier, proclaimed her skill as an events manager, hearing him praise her felt like being dipped in delicious warm honey. Pleasure spread through Lucinda, almost ameliorating the sting of his earlier rejection.

'That's very kind of you.'

'Kindness is irrelevant. It's the truth. And your stepmother is a fool to waste an asset like you.'

More pleasure, so that her face felt as if it were glowing brighter than the moon. 'She doesn't want me to be good at this,' Lucinda admitted, as puzzled by that as Thirio was.

'You said she had children of her own?'

Lucinda's eyes darted to his and then away again. 'Daughters.'

'Close in age to you?'

'Yes.'

He nodded thoughtfully. 'So she's either jealous of you, threatened by you, or both.'

Lucinda's lips parted. 'Why in the world would she be either of those things?'

He stared at her as though she'd lost her mind. 'Have you looked into a mirror lately, Lucinda?'

She blinked at him, genuinely confused, and he swore softly under his breath.

'Do you truly not realise how beautiful you are?'

Lucinda's eyes widened in confusion. 'Thirio, I've already told you, I don't need to hear—'

'Why would I lie? We've already established I'm not flattering you to get you into bed.'

Her stomach knotted at the very idea.

'Let me guess,' he continued. 'They've insulted your appearance at every turn.'

Girls with your complexion can't wear that. It's unforgiving. Your waistline looks like a spaceship. Why are your legs so disproportionate?

'They're brutally honest,' she conceded quietly, hating to relive those moments.

'If they have been unflattering towards you, that's not honesty.'

For the first time, in many years, Lucinda wondered if perhaps he was right. Maybe they had been mean to her for the sake of it. And was it possible jealousy was at the root of that? Lucinda's heart was pure kindness and, therefore, such an idea had never occurred to her.

'Thank you,' she said unevenly, a smile crossing her face as she blinked up at him. 'That's very nice of you to say.'

Where her heart had turned to sunshine and smiles, his expression was a storm cloud suddenly. 'But I'm not nice, Lucinda. You have to remember that.'

'Why do you say that? Why are you determined to act like this awful, beastly ghoul when, in actual fact, you seem like a very nice person?'

He flinched the tiniest amount, his expression shuttering as he looked down at the papers, effectively closing her off. 'Unfortunately, you don't know what you're talking about.'

Thirio felt like a top, spinning wildly out of control, and that was a sensation he hadn't known for a very long time. Not since the morning after the fire, when his body was broken and bandaged with a hangover threatening to split his head in two. And a gnawing sense of grief and disbelief that he had caused the explosion that had killed his parents.

But this loss of control was different. This was more elemental. He felt that his body was driving him down a road he didn't intend to travel. With every fibre of his being, he felt longing—longing for Lucinda, for pleasure, for laughter, for the obliteration and euphoria of sex. All things he had denied himself.

Beneath the table, he pressed a hand to his side, feeling the rough ruination of his skin through the fabric of his shirt, his touch a reminder, the scar a talisman to his guilt and fault, the reason he had forfeited his rights, long ago, to any kind of regular life.

But Lucinda's presence was dangerous.

She made him want to forget. And, worse, to forgive himself. Except, Thirio Skartos didn't deserve forgiveness. His parents' blood was on his hands, and he would have to live with that knowledge for the rest of his lonely life.

'There is one other factor we have not discussed.' He leaned back in his chair, hands hooked behind his head.

One other factor. Lucinda had been dreading this. The night had stretched, long and, she had to admit, the best night she'd had in a long time. Not for any specific reason. In fact, her nerves were all over the place. But sitting across from Thirio Skartos, she felt more *alive* than she'd felt in years. Only, *'one other factor'* spoke of an ending. Of goodbye. Of not seeing him again until closer to the wedding. The separation seemed like the dropping of a blade. He had stirred her body to fever pitch and then walked away, but those feelings hadn't disappeared. With every blink of her eyes she saw him, not as he was now but as he'd been on the terrace, face so close to hers. She felt his body, warm and strong, pressed against her, his hardness everything she'd ever needed.

'You've proposed a late summer date for the wedding, but it has to be sooner.'

'Why?'

His eyes probed hers, his hesitation only short. 'My sister is pregnant.'

Surprise shifted Lucinda's features into a broad smile. 'That's lovely news.'

He dipped his head in casual agreement. 'Her fiancé's a prince—albeit fourth in line—to a conservative country. Being visibly pregnant on her wedding day would draw the wrong kind of attention. They'd prefer to marry now.'

'I see.' Lucinda nodded thoughtfully, the change of date a hurdle she hadn't anticipated. 'How far along is she?'

'Six weeks.'

Lucinda nodded. 'Which gives us, perhaps, another six weeks.'

'Four, to be safe.'

Her eyes widened, then dropped to the comprehensive plan. It was an ambitious event. Not since her father had been at the helm had the company attempted such a thing. But this was what Lucinda wanted to do with her life, and, deep down, she knew she could pull it off—even with that tight deadline.

'Okay,' she said quietly, steeling herself for weeks of sleepless nights.

'You have asked, numerous times, why my sister asked me to organise the wedding for her. This is your answer.'

Lucinda blinked back up at Thirio's face, her heart tripping in her chest.

'She has been very sick. The pregnancy has her in bed, most days. The wedding must take place within a month, which left me to arrange it.'

Lucinda nodded slowly. 'But her husband's family? Surely they would want some say—'

'They haven't told the royal family that they're pregnant. Apparently, Erik's parents would not approve.'

Lucinda's jaw dropped in surprise and pique. 'What? How absurd. This is the twenty-first century.'

'Yes.' Thirio's eyes warred with Lucinda's. 'But they live by a different set of rules, according to my sister.' He placed a palm on the planning document, then slid it across the table to Lucinda, slowly and purposefully, but with a hint of dread, as though he were resisting what he was doing. 'I am the only person Lucinda could trust to manage the wedding planning and keep her confidence. No one can know about the baby. Understood?'

'You think I'm going to sell the secret to some tabloid or something?' she responded with a hurt grimace.

'No. But your company—'

'My stepmother,' Lucinda surmised. 'Don't worry. I don't plan on telling her about this wedding until it's over.'

Thirio considered that. 'Will that be possible?'

'Maybe not. But none of that is your problem. I will manage my stepmother, and the wedding, and I promise I'll keep Evie's secret. You need only provide the venue, Thirio. I won't bother you again.'

The words hung between them, their finality undeniable. Lucinda's stomach twisted into a billion knots, her blood gushing through her body so hard she could hear it washing inside her ears.

'If only that were true,' he responded darkly.

Hurt cascaded through her. Rejection was a blade, pressed to her side.

'It's clear that you will need to tour the castle properly, to finalise these plans. The logistics can't be organised from a distance. I'm afraid there's no alternative: you will need to return to Castile di Neve.'

CHAPTER NINE

SHE HAD FALLEN in love with the castle the first time she'd laid eyes on it, but the second time was even better. Now, there was the anticipation of seeing Thirio again, a week after his trip to London. Secondly, there was the mode of her arrival. When Lucinda had come here before, she'd been anxious after navigating the goat track of a road that led to the secluded castle. Today, Thirio had sent a private jet to bring her from London to the nearest city, and then a stunning helicopter with caramel leather seats and walnut detailing. And she had a bag with her.

A suitcase.

Evidence that this was not going to be a day-trip, or even a single night, but two nights, so that she could lockdown as many details as possible.

The prospect of forty-eight hours with Thirio—and now as an invited guest—sparkled on the horizon like diamond water.

It didn't matter how many times she told herself not to want things that were clearly not going to happen. She *did* want. Her body, in fact, craved him. Far from missing him, since that night in London, she had been overwhelmed by him. Every moment of sleep was tormented by memories of the few times they'd kissed, and the passion that had sizzled between them. She tossed and turned, even touched herself in the hope she would wake and find his hands on her body. But always, she was disappointed. Always, she was alone.

She pressed her forehead to the window of the helicopter as it began to circle lower, to the clearing just west of the castle. From this angle, she caught many details she'd not been privy to earlier. Smaller turrets, with ivy scrambling up one side and jasmine another, the flowers in full bloom as spring took hold of the mountains.

The helicopter touched down, rotor blades spinning slowly, and a moment later the pilot had come around to her door, opening it with a friendly smile and holding out a hand to help her down. She placed hers in it, but her eyes were on the castle.

Where was he?

It was the wrong time of day to see through the windows. The afternoon sun was creating a golden reflection that meant she could see the forest mirrored back to her, but no hint of Thirio. Could he see her? Was he watching?

The thought made her pulse thunder. She took a step towards the castle, and another, all the while aware of the loud clicking of the chopper's blades as they slowed down. The pilot removed her suitcase, carrying it easily a few paces behind Lucinda, leading her to a door at the back and opening it, before turning to leave with a polite nod.

Thirio was in there, somewhere. Would he continue to ignore the chemistry they shared? Or would he indulge it? And what did she want?

That was a question that didn't even need answering. She'd known what she wanted almost since the first moment she'd met Thirio, and she'd only grown more certain of her desire as they'd spent more time together.

Lucinda had only ever been with one man, and she'd been madly in love with him, or so she'd thought. Now, she wondered if she'd ever really known Beckett? Since him, there'd been no one. She'd been devastated after their relationship ended. Not because she'd lost him, but because of the manner of his betrayal. She told herself that had scared her off relationships, that it had been safer to throw herself into her work. But now, Lucinda was having second thoughts. Maybe she just hadn't met someone who was sufficiently tempting?

Thirio Skartos brought every single cell in Lucinda's body to life.

But she had other dreams. Other needs. What she wanted, more than anything, was to take back her father's company. Nothing could be allowed to come between her and that goal. No matter how consuming this crush was, it couldn't be allowed to steal her focus. This had to be the wedding of the decade. Everything needed to be perfect, and for that she'd have to concentrate on more than Thirio and his never-ending appeal.

She stepped into a room that was tiled in black and white, with pale blue cabinets against the wall. She rolled her suitcase along the tiles, stepping out of the mud room and into a larger hallway, looking left, then right, frowning, because she felt as though she'd been dropped in the middle of a forest without a map.

Just as she was wishing she'd brought a smoke beacon to signal for help, she heard footsteps on tile. Just the *sound* of his imminent approach was enough to send her pulse skittering wildly. She swallowed a groan and closed her eyes, sending out a silent prayer for strength, then opened her eyes to find Thirio filled them.

'Are you okay?' His concern was unexpected, and it did funny things to her equilibrium.

'Fine.' She forced a bright smile to her face to prove it.

'You looked like you were about to pass out.'

Was he standing really close? He occupied every single one of her senses. Even the air around them had changed, and was filled with Thirio. She breathed in and tasted him on the tip of her tongue. Her stomach dropped to her toes. 'I'm fine,' she repeated, a little less convincingly.

'Okay.' But he didn't move. Nor did she. It was as though a silent, invisible force were holding them right there. Every breath she took was mirrored back to her, his chest's gentle rise and fall drawing her gaze. She wasn't sure how long they stood like that, but eventually Thirio did what she could not, and broke the spell.

'Are you hungry?' He reached for her bag, their fingers brushing, so fireworks detonated just beneath her skin.

'Not really.'

'Then let me show you to your room.'

She fell into step beside him, her eyes scanning this new, unfamiliar part of the castle, while her body stayed resolutely focused on the man at her side. She was conscious of everything about him, and that was a form of torment.

'Where in the castle are we?' she asked, shaking her head a little, as he led them down corridors lined with ancient paintings, dimly lit and dusty smelling, that would have, at one time, or with a little care, been exquisite.

'The western towers.' He tilted her a glance. 'When the castle was first built, this outer wall was used for defence.'

'Really?'

'It was not like this then.' The smallest hint of a smile warmed his expression and her stomach lurched. She wanted him to smile more; she wanted to be the *reason* he smiled. 'Some time in the nineteenth century, the castle was overhauled. This large, open, relatively plain space was converted into a series of guest bedrooms, with some dining rooms. In the twentieth century, bathrooms were even added,' he said, his tone droll.

'I thought you'd like the view in here.' He pushed open a large timber door, gesturing for her to precede him into a room that was enormous, very old, and very beautiful. And yet, despite its perfection, Lucinda couldn't help feeling a wave of disappointment. The room she'd used last time had been so close to *his* room. She didn't have her bearings, but she couldn't help wondering if he was stashing her as far away as possible.

'It's very nice, thank you.'

She could feel his gaze on her face, watchful, intent, far too perceptive, so she turned her back on him, moving towards the window and inspecting the view. He was right—it was a stunning outlook. If she craned her neck, she could see all the way to the town at the base of the mountain pass, the little tiled roofs just specks from this distance, and in the foreground there was the magnificent forest that surrounded this castle. Though it hadn't always been this way. There were photographs on the Internet of the castle standing tall and proud, the forest trimmed back to allow the castle to draw the eye of any who cared to look. Now, it was grown over, the once grand gardens in disrepair.

And suddenly, now that she'd jumped the first hurdle and gained Thirio's permission for this plan, she began to wonder if she'd bitten off way more than she could chew. What if the castle was too run-down to be made ready for the wedding? What if the garden was too hazardous? She'd need to investigate Thirio's liability insurance before going too much further. Oh, her head was swimming with logistics, but in the midst of it all, there was a dangerous awareness of her host. Perhaps it was a good thing that he'd stowed her here, as far away from his room as the castle permitted?

Maybe it meant she'd actually get some work done?

'There is a bathroom, though it takes a while for hot water to get into the taps.'

'It's lovely,' she said quietly.

'Would you like a moment to freshen up before I show you the rest of the castle?'

Thump. Thump. Thump. Her heart was beating so hard she was sure the sound of it was reverberating around the old stone walls. He wasn't going to ditch her here. He was offering a personal tour.

'I'm okay to look around now.' She smiled up at him, her heart rushing.

His expression shifted, a mask slipping into place that kept her locked on the outside. 'Good. I need to make sure you understand which parts of the castle are off-limits. Follow me.'

Of course, it was about protecting his privacy rather than spending time with her. She shouldn't have let her hopes get raised.

Focusing on the business, she asked, 'Have you spoken to your sister about the plan?'

'Yes.'

'What did she say?'

Thirio slid her a knowing glance. 'She loved it.'

Lucinda expelled a sigh of relief. 'I'm so glad. I really hoped she would.'

'She said she could not have planned a more perfect wedding herself. She said you had thought of every detail.'

Lucinda's heart soared. It was exactly what she'd tried to do. 'And holding the wedding here? She's okay with that?'

'Why wouldn't she be?'

Lucinda considered that. 'I thought she might have doubts, because you're—'

'Ah.' He nodded slowly. 'Yes. She did. I have made no secret of the fact I like my privacy. Naturally she was concerned that opening the doors to the castle would be an inconvenience too great to bear.'

'And is it?'

'If it were, I wouldn't have agreed to it.'

'Even for your sister?'

His eyes bored into hers for several seconds, but he didn't answer her question. 'There are twenty-seven rooms in this western wing. I suggest we hold them for the royal family and their entourage. There are private dining rooms, sitting rooms, and areas where they can come to be away from the prying eyes of guests whenever they wish.'

'That's very thoughtful of you.'

'It was Evie's suggestion,' he added, something like a smile tightening his lips.

Lucinda considered him carefully as they emerged into the corridor. This time, she took in more of the details, from the ornate tiles to the delicate wallpaper, the paintings that were portraits of people who'd lived centuries ago, and brass lights that hung from the ceiling. There were not many windows, but those they passed framed a magnificent view, causing Lucinda to wonder why the renovation hadn't included making the windows bigger?

'The reason these rooms work is this private access,' he said, gesturing to the door through which Lucinda had arrived. 'It can be secured for their visit with their own people.'

'You've thought of everything.'

His frown was reflexive. 'No, Lucinda, you did. I'm only making it fit the areas of the house you didn't know about.'

The praise fanned the flames in her belly. She couldn't help but smile at him appreciatively, her eyes twinkling and her cheeks pale pink in the dusk light. His eyes held on her face for a beat too long and then his focus returned to the home.

His tour was exhaustive. The ground floor had been modernised twenty years earlier. 'My parents,' he admitted after a small pause. But it was when he showed her into the ballroom that Lucinda realised how right she'd been to fight for this.

'It's perfect,' she whispered, reaching out and pressing a hand to his forearm quite by instinct. He stiffened at the innocent contact but she didn't withdraw her touch. She couldn't. She was too overwhelmed. This truly was the most beautiful room she'd ever been in.

The space was enormous—far bigger than she'd conceptualised—with ceilings that had to be at least ten metres tall. A string of chandeliers ran down the centre, crystal and ornate, with one in the middle of the room that was at least four times as large as any of the others. Here, there was no shortage of windows. One side of the room was filled with ancient, carved glass, fine and etched, that framed views of the valley, the forest, the sky and the town in the distance, with its medieval church spire just visible from here. At the far end of the ballroom was a set of beautiful timber doors, wide and grand.

'Where do they lead?' she asked, in awe.

'I'll show you.' Was she imagining the hitch to his voice? She couldn't take her eyes off the room, the shining parquet floor an artwork in and of itself. Her fingers stayed curled around his forearm as they moved. But it was a mistake, because all she could imagine was how it would feel to be here under different circumstances. Not as a paid contractor, but as a bona fide guest, invited by Thirio. Dancing with him beneath these incomparably beautiful chandeliers, the light golden and warm, as his hand pressed to her lower back...

She bit down on her lower lip, trying to calm her racing nerves, but his proximity only made the fantasy seem more real.

When they reached the doors, he pressed a hand to one, opening it with the slightest groan courtesy of its age.

'Watch your step,' he urged, dislodging her grip on his arm, but only so that he could use that exact same arm to curve around her back, drawing her closer to him as he shepherded her out onto the most exquisite balcony. It was large enough to accommodate perhaps ten people, and reminded her of the balconies at Buckingham Palace, where the royal family would gather to wave to their people.

'It's beautiful.' But her focus was no longer on the balcony, or the view, or the sublime sunset colours streaking through the sky, painting the forest in shades of deep violet and gold. She turned to face him slowly, bravely, but also with a sense of inevitability, to find his eyes resting heavily on her face, a frown marring his lips.

Again, her hand lifted of its own accord, pressing to his shirt front, her fingers splayed wide. She stared at her fingertips a moment, before lifting her eyes to his, almost blinking away again for the sheer rush of awareness that bolted through her at his nearness.

'Thirio.' She said his name without knowing what she wanted to ask him.

His features gave little away, but he made no effort to put space between them, nor to clear her hand from his body.

'Have you—?' She hesitated, embarrassed by the question she'd been about to ask.

'Yes?'

She swallowed past a bundle of nerves in her throat. She had been silenced by uncertainty for a long time and didn't want that to be the case with Thirio. With him, Lucinda wanted to be completely herself, without fear of failure, without fear of anything. 'Have you thought about me, Thirio?'

His brows drew together, features darkening, as though her question was the last thing he'd expected. 'In what way?'

Her smile was lacking humour. 'Not the wedding planning kind of way.'

He made a noise of comprehension, his expression ambivalent. She waited, breath held, sure he was going to say 'no'. She braced herself for that disappointment, told herself it didn't matter.

But then his hand lifted, cupping her face, his thumb brushing the flesh at the side of her lips, as though willing himself not to kiss her. 'What do you think?'

'I truly don't know,' she admitted after a beat. 'I can't tell if I'm alone in what I'm feeling, or if you feel it too.'

'That's hard to believe.'

'What's that supposed to mean?'

'I've made my feelings evident.' His voice was little more than a growl. 'But I have also explained why I cannot act on them.'

She tilted her face towards his, an invitation in the parting of her lips and the gentle push of her body.

He dipped his head forward, not to be near her so much as to draw breath. But that didn't matter. The action brought his face closer to hers and

Lucinda was sick of being pushed away. Maybe it was the magic of this castle, but she felt alive with temptation and need, and she *liked* the way that felt.

'Even when it's what we both want?'

'I'm sorry that you want me,' he admitted gruffly.

'I'm not.' She had to be bold, to make him understand. 'I've only ever been with one man before, Thirio, and I was never really into him, physically. Not like this.'

Thirio's expression was tortured. That was the only word for it. He stared at her, a plea in his eyes, disbelief etched around the lines of his mouth.

'I've *never* met someone and wanted them like I do you. That's not to say I *like* you, or even have a crush on you. I'm grown up enough to know that physical desire is a whole separate ballgame to love. You don't need to worry that I'm getting unrealistic expectations. But I do desire you, Thirio. I do want you. And I guess I'm not really in the mood to ignore that, given how rare this is for me.'

He stared at her, stricken and lost, and she waited, aware that she'd just dropped a bombshell on his lap.

When he spoke, it was slowly, with consideration behind every word. 'The fact that you are so inexperienced is simply another reason for us to avoid this.'

This. He wouldn't put a label on it, but it was there, between them, an actual feeling and need.

'Why?'

He compressed his lips.

'You think because I've only ever had one lousy boyfriend before—and believe me, he was lousy—I won't be able to sleep with you and keep a level head.'

He leaned down, his forehead pressed to hers, eyes pinched shut. 'Stop.'

'Why? I didn't come here intending to say this. In fact, I came here planning to focus on the job, and not you at all. But within one minute of seeing you again, all this bubbled up inside me. It's an uncontainable desire. If you don't feel it too, then tell me. I'll respect that. But if you're going as mad with longing as I am, then, please, put us both out of our misery.'

He groaned. 'I have thought of you.' His breath fanned her face. 'I have dreamed of you. I have wanted you.' He closed his eyes, as if seeking strength. 'But you don't understand what you're asking of me.'

'I know that you want to stay here, alone and cut off from the world. I'm not offering any kind of permanent reprieve from that. When your sister's wedding is over, we'll never see one another again, I promise. My life is wrapped up in my father's company, and that's just how I want it. But we have this small window of opportunity, Thirio, and I'm here, with you, asking you to stop fighting what we both want. Just for now.'

'Damn it, Lucinda.' She braced for his rejection. She knew it was coming. She was sure of it.

But then, to her surprise and delight, he scooped her up against his chest and carried her, through the lovely timber doors, across the parquetry dance floor, and straight into her wildest fantasies.

CHAPTER TEN

HER SKIN WAS like velvet, flawless and smooth, the palest cream colour all over, except for her breasts, which were peaked in strawberry-pink, delightfully full and round, the perfect size for his hands. He held them, felt their weight, massaged them until he knew he had committed every detail to memory, then he kissed her. Hard and fast at first, befitting his need. He'd thrown off all shackles, all hesitation, and given himself over to temptation completely. It was a betrayal of the pledge he'd made the morning after his parents' deaths, and he knew he'd regret this, even at the same time he suspected he'd always feel grateful for it, and her.

She was wrong about not being a reprieve. She was. For when Lucinda was in the room, she brought sunshine and warmth and somehow that pushed back the darkness, just for a while. He could never allow the darkness to go, though. He deserved to feel it. He needed to feel it. Only in submitting to that pain could he live with what he'd done.

But for tonight, there was this. Her skin, softer than a rose bud. His hands caressed her body, his mouth tasted hers, then ran lower, teasing each nipple in turn, flicking and rolling until she was a whimpering mess beneath him. Lower still, over her flat stomach and rounded hips, holding her to the bed, pinning her beneath him as his mouth roamed lower. Slowly, sensually, tasting her, nipping her with his teeth, until he reached the pale hair at the apex of her thighs and flicked her there with his tongue.

She cried out, arching her back, but his hands were firm. When she stilled, he relinquished the grip of one, moving it instead to her legs, separating them. He gloried in the feel of her femininity beneath his fingertips, parting her for his tongue, tasting her and pleasuring her until both were almost at breaking point.

He made a growling sound against her sex then shifted his mouth to her inner thigh, pressing his lips to the flesh there and sucking, unrelenting. This was less about pleasure and more about possession. Though it was something he'd never done before, Thirio wanted to mark Lucinda, here, in one of her most private places, so that she would see it tomorrow and know that he had touched her there.

When his work was complete, he moved lower,

tasting his way down her leg, to her ankles, before standing at the foot of the bed and simply staring at her.

This was everything he had fought for six long years and yet he gloried in her presence, he revelled in his mastery of her body even while acknowledging she held a similar, if not greater, power over him. He wanted to make it last, but at the same time he needed to feel her, to bury himself inside her, to reassure himself that he wasn't dreaming.

It had been years since he'd slept with a woman, but certain instincts were ingrained. Such as needing to use a condom. That was something he didn't have here at the *castile*. Why would he? He swore under his breath in his native Greek, his heart ricocheting through his chest with disbelief.

She pushed up onto her elbows. 'Please don't stop this again.'

'I don't have any protection.' He dragged a hand through his dark hair until it spiked at strange angles. 'I haven't been with a woman in a long time. I'm out of practice.'

'You don't seem it,' she said with a soft, husky laugh. But Thirio wasn't laughing. He felt as if his body were being split in two. Could they risk not using one?

His eyes dragged up her beautiful body to her face, flushed pink to the roots of the hair.

'I—um…' She darted her gaze towards the window, where the trees sat verdant green against the dusk sky. 'I brought some.'

He wanted to scream *Hallelujah!* He wanted to laugh and praise the heavens, but, most importantly, he wanted to melt into the ground with the force of his gratitude. His reaction was proof—as though he needed any—that he really did want this to happen.

'Where?'

'In my handbag.'

'Which is?'

'In my bedroom.' She groaned, and he understood why. He'd intentionally put her in the room farthest away from him, in an attempt to prevent exactly this.

He reached for her hand, lacing their fingers together, pulling her naked form against his own. 'Come with me.' The words were a gruff command, one he hoped she wouldn't question.

She didn't.

On his own, the walk to the western towers took perhaps five minutes, but with Lucinda, it took twenty. They kissed the whole way, their hands tangling, running over one another's bodies, relishing the sensations of being free to do this, at last. It was a form of torture. By the time they finally reached the room he'd allotted for her use, his blood was raging in his body, so fast and hard he could barely hear over its thundering torrent.

'Where?' he ground out, pulling his mouth away just long enough to ask the question. She spun around, looking over her shoulder, and he followed her gaze to the bag. He moved, long strides, picking it up and tipping it onto the bed, ignoring the jumble of lipstick, pen, notepad, phone, and landing on a strip of four condoms with a bubble of relief and amusement, all rolled into one.

'Thank God for your forethought.'

'God had very little to do with it,' she quipped in response. 'It was all wishful thinking.'

He spun around to face her, holding out the condoms. 'Care to do the honours?'

Her eyes flared wide and she nodded, her fingers trembling as she took the foil square from him. She used her teeth to open it, and his eyes hungrily chased the gesture, staying on her full lower lip, right until she liberated the rubber from its wrapping and came to stand in front of him.

When she knelt down, he almost regretted suggesting this. He hadn't been with a woman for more than six years and he seriously thought he had the stamina to stand still while she touched his arousal with those beautiful hands of hers?

When her mouth connected with his fractured, ruined skin on his hip, he startled. It was not what he'd expected. Her caress was so gentle, like silk, and on a part of his body that he had long ago associated with loss and guilt and self-flagellation; it was impossible to feel her kiss and not want to recoil. It was his scar. Burned, broken skin that spoke of horrors and had no place here in this moment of unimaginable pleasure. But it was a part of him, the truth of his soul, and he could never ignore it, could never forget what he'd done. And most vitally, he could never allow himself to hurt another soul.

Her lips moved sideways, slowly, as he had done to her, and he realised the cruelty in that torture now, for he yearned for her in a way that was immediate and wild, which could barely be contained by this slow, cautious exploration. But then, her lips kissed the base of his erection, her tongue flicking at the taut flesh there, before running over him, following a dark, throbbing vein to his tip, where a bead of pleasure shimmered. She lifted her eyes to his, confusion in the depths of hers as she darted out her tongue and tasted him, moaning softly as he filled her mouth. There was nothing soft about the sound Thirio made. His response was an eruption in the room, a loud, guttural groan that bounced off the walls, filling his ears with his own surrender.

'Don't,' he ground out, reaching for her shoulders, drawing her attention to his face.

'You...don't like it?' The uncertainty in her eyes was his undoing.

'I like it, too much. I haven't slept with a woman in six years. If you do that again, this will be over.'

'For now,' she responded impishly, grinning up at him.

For now was a phrase that held such promise. He had to hold himself back from reminding her that this was not the beginning of a relationship, so much as...what? He couldn't answer that.

'Yes, for now,' he agreed, after a beat. 'And I want to lose myself in you.'

Her eyes widened and her hands lifted, holding his arousal, as if committing him to memory as he'd done with her, and then she was reaching for the condom and stretching it down his length. The slow procession was torture. At several points, he wanted to take over, but his own hands were shaking and he wasn't sure if he'd be able to achieve the result any faster.

Finally, he was sheathed, and their passion threatened to engulf them completely. He reached down, lifting Lucinda to standing, kissing her lips, parting her mouth and warring with her tongue as though his life depended on it, as their bodies meshed once more, arms tangled with arms in an effort to get closer, legs pushing between one another's legs, as they stumbled and tumbled to the bed, finally falling onto it, pens and lipsticks beneath his back as she rolled on top of him, her kiss taking over, dominating, as she straddled him hungrily.

'Hang on,' he muttered, reaching behind his back and pulling out her keys, pushing them to one side, then freeing up as much detritus as he could, swiping it from under him, uncaring when it hit the floor with a loud succession of clunks.

She laughed but only for a moment. When he settled back on the bed, she moved her mouth back to his, kissing him and tasting him, lifting her hips and bringing her womanhood closer to his arousal, teasing him with her nearness, until, finally, she wasn't teasing so much as taking him, all of him, inside. Slowly, slowly, her muscles stretching around his size, inch by inch, until, finally, he was buried deep within her, so tight and spasming that his control was almost completely shot. A sound hissed from between his teeth as he closed his eyes and let the feelings explode through him.

Hell, he wasn't going to last long. Apparently, taking care of his needs with his own hand was no substitute for actual sex.

He pushed up, rolling Lucinda to her back, staring down at her with a sense of frustration. He needed to control this. He had to be able to pleasure her without losing himself. His pride was at stake here. Thirio was not a selfish lover; he never had been. He loved making women feel good, and that hadn't changed.

Watching her face, he moved, slowly at first, then faster, all the while concentrating on the nuances of her expression, seeing what she liked most, bringing her to the edge of pleasure slowly, building it within her before pulling back, kissing her gently, relieving the pressure, then building it up again, until, finally, she tipped over, exploding in a loud, frantic, sudden wave, her muscles tightening around him until, control be damned, he was coming too, his own release almost in synch with hers, his body racked by the force of his release as he held himself above her, staring down at Lucinda without seeing her, for the brightness of the shooting stars darting across his eyelids.

He felt as though he'd run a marathon; he felt as though he were king of the world! Everything was bright and shiny and delightful. Now when he stared at Lucinda, she came back into focus, her beautiful face flushed and watchful, those full, angelic lips pouted into a natural smile, her bare décolletage begging for his attention. He dropped his head and kissed her there, feeling the frantic racing of her pulse beneath his lips, tasting her salty perspiration and finding that even that was an aphrodisiac. His arousal jerked inside her, and she made a rasping sound.

'I appreciate your enthusiasm,' she whispered into his ear, so he tilted his face and found her watching him with the most angelic expression.

His gut twisted. This was a betrayal in every sense of the word. And yet, he'd made himself clear to her. She wasn't expecting anything from this, besides sex. How could either of them resist this? Why had he bothered trying? Not for six years had he been tempted, but there was something about Lucinda Villeneuve that had turned his pledge on its head. It went beyond the fact she'd arrived here unannounced and gone toe to toe with him. This was more complicated, more elemental. Completely unavoidable.

'That was amazing.'

He lifted a single dark brow. 'There's room for improvement,' he conceded, though his body felt pretty bloody great.

'Oh, really?' She ran a finger down his cheek, towards his lips. 'What would you change?'

'For one thing, I'd have the stamina to give you more than one orgasm.'

'Not just one orgasm,' she corrected. 'A mind-blowing, life-altering orgasm.'

'Ah.' He nodded with mock seriousness. 'Then at least three of those.'

'Three?' she repeated incredulously. 'I can't even imagine.'

'You won't have to imagine.' He turned his head quickly, capturing her finger between his teeth and biting down on it, so she laughed. 'Next time.'

The words floated between them, a silent promise that lifted her skin with goosebumps.

'You certainly know how to set the bar high,' she said after a moment.

It felt so good to be lying naked with her. He wanted to stay there all evening, until he was ready to take her again, but that was all the more reason he had to move. Oh, he'd succumbed to this, absolutely, but he wasn't ready to lose all of himself. There still had to be an element of control and separation.

He pulled out of her with regret, standing and turning his back so he could dispose of the condom in a wastepaper basket, before coming back to the side of the bed. She was still lying where he'd left her, completely spent. He studied her, delighting in his effect on her, knowing he should pull her to standing and draw her away from the bed, return to the business she'd come here to do.

But greater forces were at play, and instead Thirio flopped back beside her, albeit with a good two feet of space between them. He propped onto his side, facing her, and a moment later Lucinda did the same thing, echoing his body language. It was almost impossible to lie there and not reach out to touch her, but Thirio wanted to challenge himself, and so he stayed where he was, with all the appearance of being at ease even when a coil was beginning to wind inside his belly, tighter and tighter, building pressure as though he hadn't just had the mother of all releases.

'Have you really not slept with a woman in six years?'

'No.'

Her lips quirked downward. 'I'm surprised.'

And though he could understand her surprise, he shrugged and said, 'Why? You shouldn't believe everything you read on the Internet.'

'Well, pictures don't lie,' she said quietly, mulling this over. 'And there are a lot of photos of you with a lot of different women.'

Yes, that was true. 'It was another life.'

Sympathy darkened her amber eyes. Damn it. He didn't want to do this. He didn't want Lucinda, of all people, to feel sorry for him. He was so sick of the way people looked at him, and to have her turn into one of *them* was the last thing he wanted.

'My sex life is not interesting,' he said darkly. 'I would much rather discuss yours.'

'Or the lack thereof?'

'Yes,' he agreed. 'That is a much greater mystery. How is it possible that a woman like you has not had more than one boyfriend?'

She lifted a hand to her throat, as if looking for something. He remembered the necklace he'd seen on the first day, diamond on a fine silver chain.

'I can't say.'

'Because it is a secret?'

'No, because there's not really any particular reason.'

His eyes narrowed. 'What happened to your claim that you are always honest?'

Her lips parted in surprise. 'I'm—I am being honest.'

'No, you're hiding something from me.'

She looked as though she was about to deny it and he waited, his expression giving nothing away. But then, she sighed softly and focused her gaze on the bedspread between them. 'It was not a good breakup. I guess I lost a lot of confidence when he left me. And relationships are hard, you know? You have to put yourself out there and be vulnerable to another person. You have to trust someone else not to hurt you, and, after Beckett, I just wasn't able to do that again.'

Thirio had a burning curiosity. He wanted to understand everything about this Beckett, including how he could be so stupid as to treat a woman like Lucinda badly enough that she'd be gun-shy of all relationships.

'What did he do to you?'

The tone of his voice drew her gaze. She furrowed her brow, adding complexity and interest to a face that was already far too mesmerising. 'He fell in love with someone else.'

'Someone you knew?'

Wariness flashed in her eyes. Surprise too. 'Yes.'

'Someone you trusted?'

Her lips pulled sideways. 'I wouldn't say that.' Lucinda's long, elegant fingers moved between them, plucking at the bedspread. 'One of my stepsisters, Sofia.'

'The woman I met at your office?'

'No, that was Carina. She's not—quite as bad as Sofia.'

Thirio had run the gamut of emotions in his life. He'd known delirium and joy as a boy, and careless, giddy happiness as a teenager and then the flipside to that, incomparable loss and grief as a young man, but he wasn't sure he'd ever known an emotion quite like the one pummelling him from the inside out. It was a mix of protectiveness and angry disbelief. 'Tell me about these women, *agape mou*.' The endearment slipped out before he could stop it, words he'd never said to a woman in his life, for the simple reason he'd heard his father say them to his mother so many times, they seemed almost to belong to his parents.

She opened her mouth, then closed it, sighing softly. 'What do you want to know?'

'You have said your stepmother mistreated you. I gather your stepsisters were just as bad?'

'No, no one could be.' She responded quickly and with no artifice, so he knew that whatever torment her stepmother had put Lucinda through must have been truly awful. 'I can't blame my stepsisters. They're by-products of their upbringing and my stepmother is not a kind woman. They were never taught to see the goodness in the world, nor in people. They perceive life through a prism of what they can get, not what they can give.'

Her words spoke volumes about her own outlook, but then, he already understood this facet of Lucinda. From the moment she'd arrived, she'd lobbied hard to give Evie her dream wedding. She'd fought hard for a woman she'd never met, because of the connection of being without parents. How deeply did this experience define Lucinda?

'Whereas you prefer to make people happy.'

Her eyes widened. 'What's wrong with that?'

He put his hand over hers, staring at the visage they made. 'Nothing.' His voice was hoarse. He cleared his throat, focusing the conversation back on less tenuous ground. 'Did you love this man?'

She bit down on her lower lip and his abdomen tightened. 'I thought I did. Looking back, I think I was just desperate to be in love, and, more importantly, to be loved by someone in return.'

'After your father died, was there no one besides your stepmother who could have raised you? Grandparents? Aunts and uncles?'

'No. No one.'

'I'm sorry,' he said with sincerity.

Lucinda's smile was uneven, a failed attempt at the gesture. 'I didn't really want to move out, anyway. It's the only home I've ever known, and to think of my stepmother and stepsisters living there, without me, without Dad.' She shook her head, her eyes shifting as though searching for words. 'It was like a bomb had gone off right in the middle of my life,' she said quietly, with no idea that she was speaking to someone who'd lived through an actual explosion, and knew exactly what a detonation sounded like, smelled like, tasted like. He tried to push away the memories, seared into his brain, and focus instead on her words. She'd invoked an expression, that was all. 'One minute it was just Dad and me. The next, he'd fallen madly in love and was getting married.'

'And you supported him in this.'

'Of course,' she responded instantly. 'He was my father and I wanted him to be happy. I thought she'd make him happy.'

'And did she?'

Lucinda hesitated. 'I don't have enough experience of relationships to say for sure. Perhaps it was a different kind of happiness. More complex, maybe more rewarding? I don't know.'

He lifted his hand to her cheek, pushing some hair behind her ear then returning it to her hand. Just the simple contact stirred heat in his veins, renewed desire. 'Did they argue?'

'Not really. They just didn't seem to "click". Maybe I had romanticised ideas of what a great relationship should be like. I was only fifteen and, to that point, had watched a heck of a lot of Disney movies and read my fill of romance novels,' she said with a soft smile. 'I thought he'd stepped into a fantasy and that our life was going to be everything I'd always wanted. A real family, at last.' She shook her head. 'But instead, I kind of...'

'Yes?' he prompted, when she tapered off into silence.

'I sort of just lost my dad, from the moment they were married. All of the little rituals we had stopped overnight. My stepmother seemed to resent anything that he and I shared. I wanted to include them, but she preferred to start new traditions.'

'That's insensitive.'

'Yes.' Lucinda's features tightened, her face showing pain, so he wanted to ease it, to push it away for her. He'd known enough of those torturous inner feelings to wish to free her from them for life. 'I don't know what happened to my stepmother to make her the way she is. I used to want to try to know, to understand her and even help her, but...'

'She pushed you too far.'

Her eyes flared wide at his perceptive comment. 'Yes,' she agreed softly. 'Now I just want her out of my life.' She flipped her hand over, capturing his, her fingers brushing the skin between his thumb and forefinger. 'I wish her well. I want her to be happy. I just don't want her to be anywhere near me.'

'And your stepsisters?'

'Them too.'

He could imagine what it took for a woman like Lucinda, who was all kindness and goodness, to express such feelings about anyone. 'How old were you when this man left you for your stepsister?'

'Nineteen. It feels like a lifetime ago.'

'Did they stay together?'

She shook her head. 'It was never really about that. Sofia seduced him just to take him away from me. I had something good in my life, I was happy and felt loved for the first time in a long time, and I guess she didn't like that.'

He bit back the curse that came to mind. 'What about him?'

'He was...not the man I thought him to be. He didn't even fight for what we shared. I meant nothing to him,' she added, the last words said so calmly and yet he felt the tension emanating from them, the importance of that phrase to her being, in some way.

'And so you swore off men and relationships?'

'It wasn't so dramatic as that.' A smile tugged at her lips and something in the region of his heart glowed warm. 'More than anything, I just couldn't imagine getting close to someone, only to have them leave me again. So I focused on the business.'

'And that became your life.'

'Yes,' she agreed. 'And it's enough for me. It's all I want, Thirio. It's all I'll ever want.'

CHAPTER ELEVEN

THAT HE'D SET up a state-of-the-art office for her shouldn't have surprised Lucinda. He had told her, right from their first meeting, that he was detail-orientated. But it was beyond her expectations to have these facilities at her disposal.

It was the perfect space to work, and yet there was one problem.

She was distracted. For every ten minutes she spent emailing contractors and tying down details of the wedding, her mind wandered to Thirio, and the way they'd come together the night before, as though driven by forces much greater than they could understand. Passion had hummed and zipped around them like a cord, tying them together. There had been no escaping their love-making. It was inevitable. And perfect.

A smile touched her lips and she leaned back in her chair, running her eyes over the computer screen without really focusing. She'd been at it for hours, and, though she hadn't achieved as much as she'd wanted, she was confident the wedding was on track. The biggest items had been ticked off—the caterers were world class, the menu she'd selected carefully put together to appeal to all palates and tastes. The musicians had been booked and the photographer she'd spoken to had set aside a photoshoot for *Vogue* magazine to come and capture the wedding. Everything was going to be perfect.

A smile pulled at her lips, a true smile, born of absolute, untouched happiness. And hope. Because this wedding was the gateway to her dreams—she was so close to being able to buy the business. But it was more than that. She felt hope because of what she'd shared with Thirio. She wasn't stupid enough to think that sleeping together was the start of a meaningful relationship, and yet it *had* meant something to her. It was the breaking down of a wall she'd built around her heart. She didn't trust Thirio in the sense that she wanted to spend the rest of her life with him, but she had put her faith in him for this short while, and that was a big step for Lucinda. Maybe she wasn't as closed off to relationships as she'd come to believe.

His intrusion was not unwelcome. Nor was it really a surprise. It was as though she'd manifested his arrival.

'I brought you coffee.' He placed the cup on the edge of the desk, remaining where he was, arms crossed, eyes skimming her face in that intense way he had. Her heart trembled.

'Thank you. Coffee is always welcome.' She reached for it, inhaling the fragrance before taking a deep sip. After they'd made love the night before, they'd eaten dinner—toasted sandwiches—then gone back to bed. Lucinda hadn't slept much and she was tired now. She stifled a yawn then sent him an apologetic smile.

'How's it going?' He nodded towards the computer screen.

'Everything's on track.' She ticked off the list of professionals she'd hired. 'Our firm's worked with all of them previously. They're the best in the business.'

'I trust you.'

She startled—the words expressing so perfectly the thoughts she'd had moments earlier—then blinked away. He only meant that he trusted her to manage the wedding.

'I've prepared a brief note, to update you as to my progress.' She reached for the printout she'd made only half an hour earlier. 'Ordinarily, it would go to your sister, but as you're handling all the logistics…'

'I'll email it to her,' he said, taking a photo of the document, clicking a couple of buttons then returning his focus to her face. 'She's been a bit better the last couple of days. She'd love to see it.'

'Has she been able to organise a dress?' Lucinda enquired sympathetically.

'There is a designer attached to the Nalvanian palace,' he said with a nod. 'That's taken care of.'

'Of course.' Lucinda's eyes drifted to the view beyond the window. It was such a beautiful castle. What a shame that it should be a prison rather than a home. She frowned, the thought coming to her unprompted, and yet she realised that it was accurate. That was how Thirio used this place: the walls kept him locked away from the world, and the world locked away from him.

The idea of that propelled her to stand and move to him, to press her hands to his chest and stare up at his face. The air around them grew thick, their awareness impossible to fight now that they'd been together. Their bodies were in sync, hearts beating in unison.

'Have you worked enough for now?' he growled, arms behind her back, drawing her closer to him, so she felt the stirring of his attraction through the fabric of her dress.

Her eyes widened, lifting to his in time to see a mocking smile on his lips. 'The coffee might have been a ruse,' he said with a non-apologetic shrug.

'Ahh...' She grinned right back at him. 'But an excellent one.' She moved one hand to reach for the cup, taking two big sips before returning it to the edge of the desk. 'I'm quite tired after last night.'

'Are you?' He scanned her face. 'Do you need to go back to bed for a bit?'

Heat spread through her like lava. 'Yes.' She nodded slowly. 'But not to sleep.'

Thirio had travelled in helicopters since he was a young boy. He was intimately familiar with the *thwop-thwop-thwop* noise of the blades, and particularly when they drew close to Castile di Neve. But in his drowsy state, it took him a moment to place the noise, and then to realise what it meant. He shifted, dislodging Lucinda so she woke, blinking at him as if from a very deep dream, then smiled, happiness and contentment so obvious on her beautiful face.

'Someone's here,' he explained, nodding towards the window of his room, which now showed a dark speck growing closer.

'Maybe it's just flying overhead.'

'The trajectory is wrong for that.' He squinted a little, recognising the golden emblem on the side of the aircraft. 'It's my sister.'

'Your sister?' Lucinda gawked, her perfectly relaxed aura disappearing. 'Coming *here*?'

He stayed where he was, bemused by her reaction. 'It does happen, from time to time. As you so wisely reminded me the day we met, this is her home too.'

'I should never have spoken to you like that,' she muttered apologetically, pushing out of bed and hurriedly pulling on underwear. The helicopter blades grew louder.

'You were right,' he said. 'And what is the matter? You're acting as though you've been caught with your hand in the cookie jar.'

Her fingers trembled a little as she slid into the dress he'd enjoyed removing hours earlier.

'She's my client.' Lucinda pulled a face.

'Technically, that's me.'

'Well, yes, *technically*,' Lucinda agreed, rolling her eyes. 'But really, it's Evie I want to impress.'

'Because I'm already impressed enough?'

She laughed. 'You're incorrigible.' She was fully dressed, but it didn't change the fact that she still looked as though she'd been being ravished for hours. A conclusion she evidently came to herself when her eyes landed on their reflection in the mirror. 'Oh, gawd,' she squawked, bending down and grabbing his jeans then tossing them across the room at him. 'Get dressed.' When he didn't move, she pushed her hands together. 'Ple-e-e-ease.'

His laugh surprised them both. It was a natural, deep rumble, true mirth in its tone. 'Relax.' He shook his head. 'She doesn't bite.'

'I just don't want her to think this is how I got the job.'

'I'll happily tell her that you broke in and refused to leave until I'd acquiesced.'

'Thi-ir-io-o-o-o…' she moaned, finger-combing

blonde hair over her shoulder with one hand, while the other licked her thumb then wiped clean the smudges of make-up around her eyes. 'Please don't.'

'Relax,' he repeated. 'It's going to be fine.'

'Easy for you to say,' she said with a shake of her head. 'Your whole future isn't riding on the next fifteen minutes of your life.'

'And neither is yours. You'll get paid no matter what my sister thinks of you.'

Lucinda's eyes widened, and hurt showed in their stunning amber depths. 'This isn't about money,' she said stiffly. He frowned, because, actually, it was. She needed money to buy her father's business back, and money was no issue for Thirio. In fact, he was tempted to give it to her now so she could get the ball rolling.

'Then what is it about?' he asked, gently, not wanting to scare her off.

'This is my first proper commission. I've done the hard yards on a lot of events in my time, but this is the first job I've landed on my own, the first job I'm solely responsible for. Your sister's happiness is a huge part of the success criteria. I want her to be happy—no, thrilled—with what I've arranged. It's important to me.'

Then it was important to him too. He didn't say the words. They felt wrong, and as if they might give her a misleading impression about their relationship, and yet he felt them, deep in his bones.

'Okay, okay,' he said instead, shaking his head ruefully. 'But you'd better go and choose a different dress if you don't want her to know how we've been spending our time.'

Lucinda frowned then turned to the mirror, her fingers lifting to her neck where the edge of a love bite was just visible. 'Thirio!' she squawked again. 'You are…'

'Incorrigible. You've already said that. But by my estimate, you've got five minutes before Evie walks in the door, at most.'

'Argh!' She turned and ran towards the door, in such a hurry that she jammed her hip into the bedpost as she passed it. She pressed her fingers to the spot.

'I'll kiss it better later,' he called, half laughing, to her retreating back.

At the door, she turned to face him. 'You'd better,' she muttered, smiling. And then, 'Thank you for everything. That—' her eyes fell to the bed '—was wonderful.'

Evie arrived alone, which, given her status, was very rare these days. 'I gave my guard the slip,' she said with an innocent blink of turquoise eyes. 'They fuss even more than you do.' At just over five feet tall, Evie had to stand on her tiptoes to kiss her older brother's cheek. 'How are you, darling?'

He didn't dare answer honestly. In that moment,

he felt as if he were on top of the goddamned world. But if Evie knew the reason for his unusual ebullience, she'd obsess over keeping Lucinda in his life, and that wasn't possible. Thirio was already breaking the pledge he'd made to himself. But at least it was temporary. In a matter of days, or weeks at most, things would return to normal, and for the rest of his life he would be alone, grieving his parents, paying penance for his role in their deaths. And that penance would be even more meaningful if it meant denying himself Lucinda.

'I'm fine,' he responded, his tone suitably glowering as the recollection of his guilt brought a storm cloud over his newly cheery mood.

'You look well.' She nodded her approval. 'Shall we sit on the terrace?'

'Why are you here?'

She laughed. 'Charming. Can't I come just to visit my big brother?'

'Of course you can.' He waved away her joke, trying to tamp down on his impatience. Wanting to be alone with Lucinda didn't give him the right to be rude to his sister. He softened his tone. 'How are *you* feeling, more to the point?' She looked slim, and pale. He met her concern with his own.

'Actually, I'm okay. I've eaten breakfast these last four days, so that's something. Still just a piece of toast and half a banana, but that's better than nothing.'

'It's not enough.' He frowned. 'Is your doctor any good?'

'Apparently, she's the best in Nalvania.'

'Then let me find you the best in the world,' Thirio insisted. 'Nalvania is a small country—'

'With excellent healthcare,' she assured him, shaking her head affectionately. He'd blinked and suddenly his younger sister had grown into a beautiful, confident, self-assured princess-in-waiting. 'I'm okay, Thirio. The doctors are not worried.'

'You're too thin.'

'Gee, thanks,' she muttered. 'What's got into you? You're even grouchier than usual.'

He glowered, unable to answer her question honestly. He'd been wrenched out of bed with a beautiful woman—the first lover he'd taken in six years. Damned straight he was cranky at the intrusion.

'The reason I came is to discuss this.' She brandished her phone.

He focused on the screen, recognising Lucinda's wedding details. 'Is there a problem?'

'Far from it. I'm overjoyed. Everything here is so perfect, Thirio, I can't believe it. It's as though this woman has tunnelled right into my subconscious and pulled out my innermost thoughts and wishes. The wedding is going to be everything I could ever want.'

And despite the fact he had absolutely no right,

pride puffed Thirio's chest. Not personal pride, but a sense of pride for Lucinda, and for the work she'd done. Now that he knew more about her, and understood the adversity she'd faced to accomplish what she had, he was even happier that she'd been able to so perfectly anticipate Evie's needs.

'I'd like her number so I can call and thank her.'

'You can thank her in person.'

'What do you mean?'

'She's here.'

'Here?' Evie stared at him as though he'd said something quite ludicrous. 'At the *castile*?'

Thirio laughed, her incredulity not hard to understand. 'Well, she does have to organise rather a major event.'

'Yes, but still,' Evie said with a small shake of her head. 'I didn't realise you'd be…'

'Yes?'

'I thought—' Evie laughed, then mock-punched Thirio's arm. 'Stop making fun of me. You know what I'm getting at. You *hate* people. You particularly hate having people in your personal space.'

'And yet I agreed for your wedding to be here.'

Evie was quiet, chewing on that a moment. 'Why *did* you agree to this?' Her eyes probed his. 'I know you must hate the idea.'

He nodded slowly. 'My first reaction was to say no. But then I read the plan and I knew how happy it would make you. There is nothing I want more than your happiness, Evie.' What he didn't add, but they both understood, was that he felt an obligation to deliver that happiness to her, after what he'd taken away.

'But at what cost?' she murmured. 'I don't want you to suffer.'

'I'll cope,' he drawled. 'It's one night.'

'But two days.'

'I'll cope,' he repeated firmly. 'Stop worrying and start enjoying.' His edict was followed by a knock on the door jamb of the living room and, a moment later, Lucinda ducked her head around. He stood very still. In fact, it was as though his body had been turned to rock. All he could do was stare at her. Gone was the woman he'd just been making love to. In her place stood a stunning, confident, smiling professional, wearing a silk blouse and knee-length skirt, her hair braided over one shoulder.

'Hello. You must be Evie.' Lucinda barely looked at Thirio.

'And you must be my guardian angel!' Evie responded with a soft laugh. 'Honestly, I don't know how you did this.'

'It's my job.' Lucinda shrugged modestly. 'But I'm very happy that you're pleased with the progress.'

'Pleased? I'm in awe. You've thought of everything, right down to your suggestion that guests make donations to the Nalvanian Childhood Literacy fund rather than giving us presents. After all, what more do we need?'

'I know it's a cause that's close to your heart.'

'But *how* do you know?' Evie responded with obvious disbelief. 'It's as though you're living in my mind.'

'I read a lot of interviews,' Lucinda confided with a hint of pink in her cheeks. 'That might seem a bit creepy, but I find it's the best way to get to know a client and work out how to help them.'

'On the contrary, I think it's genius. On other occasions, I've had to spend days being questioned and going over proposals and I just couldn't stomach it this time. Which is why I handed the tedium to Thirio. You've saved us both a lot of effort.'

'It's my pleasure,' Lucinda promised, her eyes briefly flicking to Thirio, who met her response with a small grin. He couldn't help it. Inwardly, he corrected her: it was *both* of their pleasure. 'Would you like me to go through it all with you?' Lucinda offered.

'That's exactly why I'm here!' Evie clapped her hands together, glowing with happiness and vitality. That brought joy to his heart, but it was immediately followed by a rush of guilt, because their mother deserved to see her like this. He'd deprived them all of so much. 'Shall we start in the ballroom?'

'Absolutely.' Lucinda turned to face him. 'Thirio? Did you want to join us?'

He was frowning, and not listening properly.

'Thirio?' Evie waved her hand in his face. 'Are you coming?'

'No.' His response was quick. Panic was rising inside him, the familiar rush of adrenalin something he'd become used to over the years. It always happened when he thought of their parents. 'You go ahead. I have work to catch up on.'

'It's a weekend, you know,' Evie reminded him, but good-naturedly, so he offered a tight smile.

'You'll have more fun without me. Go. Enjoy yourself.'

'Is he being unbearably rude?' Evie asked, when they were alone.

Lucinda jerked her gaze to Evie. 'Who?'

'My brother,' Evie said gently. 'It's okay, you don't have to protect him. I know what Thirio's like.'

Lucinda contemplated that. The first day she'd met Thirio, he'd been beastly, but it had been a long time since she'd seen that side of him. 'He's okay, actually.'

'You're very tolerant. Or perhaps very polite. Probably both.' Evie smiled. 'In any event, thank you for putting up with him. He's got a heart of gold, deep down. It's just *very* deep down, and not many people ever get to see it.' She frowned. 'In fact, I'm probably the only one who believes that.'

I believe it, Lucinda added inwardly, while nodding politely. 'A marquee will be erected over there.' She stopped walking and pointed towards a window. There was a large flat area of grass, with a stunning view of pine trees and wildflowers. 'A carpet, made locally from recycled wool, will cover the ground, preserving guests' shoes. The chairs will be sourced from the attic—did you know there's over two hundred chairs from the early twentieth century there?'

'I forgot. How did you find them?' Evie said with obvious surprise.

'I went exploring yesterday,' Lucinda said, glossing over the fact that Thirio had given her a tour of the castle. 'They're so beautiful. Classic art deco, they'll look wonderful.'

Evie's smiled was tinged with nostalgia. 'My parents used to host New Year's Eve parties here. Those are the chairs they used.' Her eyes were suspiciously moist, but she blinked quickly then smiled. 'It's good you found them. I really do want to avoid the appearance of extravagance,' Evie said as they continued their progress towards the ballroom. 'That's what I loved about your proposal. Everything is thoughtful, repurposed, meaningful, with just enough special touches to reassure traditionalists that it's a royal wedding.' She pulled a face as she said the last two words.

'I imagine there's a lot of pomp in your life?' Lucinda enquired thoughtfully.

'It's not so bad. As the fourth son, Erik has

no expectation of becoming King. It's the media that intrudes, and we cannot appear ungrateful for their attention, so it's a delicate balance.'

They entered the ballroom and Evie sighed heavily. 'I've always loved it here.'

'And yet, you don't come often?'

Evie turned to look at Lucinda, appraising her for a moment before shaking her head. 'No. It's my brother's home.'

'I get the impression you two are very close.'

'We love one another a lot, but that isn't the same thing as being close. I don't think Thirio will ever let anyone close,' she added, then shook her head. 'But that is not your burden. I shouldn't have said anything.'

'It's okay,' Lucinda said gently, a hint of guilt in the words, because the last thing she wanted to do was pump Thirio's sister for information about him. 'Anyone associated with your wedding has signed an ironclad confidentiality agreement, so whatever you say will stay between us.'

'Oh, in that case, we should grab a couple of chairs, we could be here for hours,' she joked. 'I don't mean to make it sound so bad. Thirio and I message often. I know he has my best interests at heart. But you've probably gathered from the way he lives that Thirio is a recluse. He closes himself off from the world, and that includes me. I come here when I can. Once or twice a year. But I know he is only tolerating my company, and I can't quite bear that.' Sadness made the words husky. 'I don't overstay my welcome.'

'I'm very sorry to hear it,' Lucinda replied, her own heart heavy with grief at the picture Evie was painting.

But wasn't it the exact same picture Lucinda was at the centre of? True, Thirio had been very accommodating on this trip, but that was temporary. Lucinda felt the same as Evie, in many ways: chiefly, that she could not overstay her welcome. Having already been subjected to Thirio when he was cold and dismissive, she hated the thought of being on the receiving end of that treatment again. And invariably she would be, when he decided that the time had come to end their fling.

Which was why she had to keep it light and leave as soon as her work was completed. She would take a page from Evie's book, and leave Thirio before she'd overstayed her welcome.

And just like that, all her old insecurities were back, curdling in her belly, so she found it hard to concentrate. But she forced herself to focus, enough to complete the tour, and to ask Evie the handful of questions she had to ensure she'd checked off her list.

'The seating plan is mine to worry about,' Evie said as they concluded their discussion. 'Protocol has to be observed, so someone from Erik's staff will oversee the guest list and work out the most diplomatic place to seat everybody.' She tapped her pen against the edge of the table. 'As for Thirio, there's someone I'd like him to meet.' She flashed Lucinda a conspiratorial grin. 'A girl-friend of mine, from Nalvania. He hasn't been seeing anyone for—well, a long time, but I think he might be ready. After all, he's agreed to host the wedding here, which is a huge step forward for him.'

Lucinda smiled kindly, used to concealing her innermost thoughts, and particularly used to concealing any hint of pain she was feeling. But the truth was, Evie's casual mention of a friend she wanted to set up with Thirio was like a knife in Lucinda's heart. Why should it be? Thirio wasn't her boyfriend. They'd made no promises to one another. And yet the idea of him being with another woman was anathema to Lucinda. She couldn't even contemplate it.

'Will you come to the wedding, Lucinda?' Evie asked, clear eyes on Lucinda's face, reminding her in that moment of Thirio and his very direct stare.

'I will be coming,' Lucinda responded with a professional smile. 'I'll be in the background, making sure everything runs smoothly.'

'Surely you have staff for that? I meant for you to attend as my guest. It feels like the least I can do, after the perfection you've accomplished.'

'It's my job,' Lucinda responded softly. 'And believe me, I'm much more comfortable fading into the background.'

Evie frowned, but didn't push the point. 'Well, if you change your mind, please do come. I'd love to have you there.'

'That's very kind.' Lucinda knew she'd never accept the invitation. Thirio might have made her feel as though she were on top of the world, but she was well aware that it was temporary.

When she returned to London, and the office, reality would swallow her whole again, and her stepmother and stepsisters would be reminding her of her flaws and faults as reliably as day followed night. This weekend was a fantasy. A small bubble separate from the rest of time and place, her own little nirvana on earth, but it would not last. All bubbles burst eventually.

CHAPTER TWELVE

SHE HAD TOLD herself she wouldn't ask, but as they lay on the rooftop terrace of one of the turrets, limbs entwined, the softest blanket beneath them, a spider's web of stars twinkling against the black velvet of the dawn sky, Lucinda was driven to throw caution to the wind. She kept her head pressed to Thirio's chest, listening to the steady, heavy thudding of his heart, as her finger chased the texture of his chest, feeling every knot.

'Was this from the accident?'

It was impossible not to feel how he stiffened, his body radiating tension.

'You don't have to answer. I didn't mean to pry.'

'Your curiosity is natural,' came his clipped, closed-off response. And it was such a harsh reminder of the way he'd been that first day they met that she felt as though she were teetering on the edge of a very tall building. She tried to steady her breathing but the truth was, after the intimacies they'd shared, and the way she'd relaxed with him over these past two days, going

back to that cold, closed-off man was the last
thing she wanted.

'But you don't want to talk about it.' Already,
Lucinda was pulling her barriers back into place,
telling herself she didn't care if he rejected her,
because he wasn't the first person. But the truth
was, her heart was heavy and she couldn't imagine being in the same room with Thirio and having him treat her with the coldness of a stranger.

'No.' The word was gruff, torn from his chest.
'But as I said, your curiosity is natural.'

She stayed very still.

'It wasn't an accident.' The words dropped like
stone between them.

They made no sense. 'What do you mean?'

'The night my parents died. It was no accident.'

'I've read the papers. They all say—'

'My parents were very rich, with powerful
friends. They made sure the fire was reported in
a specific way. But it was not an accident.'

She kept her ear to his chest, running her fingers over the flesh again, slower, as though she
could heal his hurt and heart with her touch. 'Then
what happened?'

'Are you sure you want to know?'

'Only if you want to tell me.'

He expelled another deep breath and this time,
she pushed up to look at him.

'It is not a matter of wanting to tell you,' he said
after a long pause. 'But it is a part of who I am.

Somehow, I don't mind you knowing, even when it will change everything.'

She waited, without speaking.

'It was the night before my father's birthday. I should have stayed home—my mother begged me not to go out. But that was what I did back then. Pointless, indulgent, selfish existence. I partied as though there were no tomorrow. I blew through tens of thousands of dollars a night. I drank too much, had indiscriminate sex, shallow friendships. I had no responsibilities and used to think I was glad.'

'I can't imagine you ever behaving like that.'

'I am not the same as I was then.'

'No.' This she'd already gathered.

'I came home in the early hours of the morning, wasted and famished. I decided to cook some bacon and set the stove going, emptying my pockets out on the bench beside it. I went upstairs to take a shower, then fell asleep. The next thing I knew, the earth beneath me was shaking.' He spoke without stopping, the words tripping over each other to get out, as though he had to relive them in this order, without a break, now that he'd started. 'There had been an explosion. It woke me, and Evie. I stumbled downstairs, to find the whole level engulfed in flames. I could hear my mother crying out. She was still alive. I just had to get to her. But there was Evie, too, and in that moment, I needed to make a decision. Evie was terrified of fire. She was crying upstairs. I ran back and got her, carrying her out, before returning to my parents. I was still drunk, Lucinda. I wasn't thinking straight, it was instincts alone that were making me act. I ran into the fire, a shirt wrapped around my face, trying to get to them. A beam fell on me. I was trapped, flames were everywhere, but somehow, I managed to push it off me and keep going. But there was too much fire. By the time I got to their room, it was hotter than the sun. I couldn't go in. I wanted to. Even now, recounting this to you, I wonder if it was really so bad. If I couldn't have pushed through and got to them. But they were already dead. I will never forget the sight of my mother on the ground, Lucinda. And all because I had to go out and get hammered, like every other night of my pointless goddamned life.'

'Oh, Thirio.' Her cheeks were wet. 'That's still an accident.'

'I put my cigarette lighter on the edge of the stove. I basically created a bomb. Yes, it was an accident, but it was also entirely my fault. This was preventable.'

Sadness welled in her chest, for so many reasons. 'And all this time, you've lived with this guilt?' she asked, pushing up so she could see him better. He stared straight ahead, his eyes fixed on the stars above them. 'All this time you've blamed yourself?'

'Who else is to blame?'

She shook her head. 'You didn't mean to cause the fire. Accidents happen.'

'And if I had broken a vase or even crashed a car, I might see it your way. But I killed my mother and father. I deprived Evie of her parents. I destroyed our family. For years I wished I had died too. It was only Evie that kept me going. I couldn't leave her.'

'Oh, Thirio, don't say that. You have so much to offer. You parents would want you to live your life.' She hesitated, not sure if she was going to ruin everything, but judging that it was more important to help him than to preserve their status quo. 'And not like this. They would want you to live your life properly and fully, to find a way to be happy. You cannot keep yourself in stasis for ever, and, what's more, you don't deserve that.'

'I deserve to rot in hell,' he muttered. 'If you could only know the kind of person I was back then. Selfish, spoiled, entitled—'

'And young,' she said quietly. 'You were still a boy, Thirio, in your early twenties.'

'It doesn't matter. Nothing you say will change this. I killed my parents, and I will live with that knowledge for as long as I live.'

'And you will stay here, away from people and fun and friends, hidden away, miserable, soaking in your grief?'

'What would you suggest as an alternative?

Draw a line in the sand under my parents' deaths and kick up my heels as though it never happened?'

'Don't be facetious,' she said softly, reproachfully, so his gaze slid sideways to hers. 'I'm not saying you can ignore your pain, nor that you should. But you have to find a way to live with it, as a part of you, rather than shutting down completely.'

'Thank you for the advice.' There wasn't a hint of gratitude in the words. 'But this is the approach that's working for me.'

'Is it really working?' She quietly reflected on that, pulling apart his sentiment. 'And this is why you've pledged not to have sex?'

'Why should I get to enjoy my life when I deprived them of theirs? When I deprived Evie of her beloved mother and father? Going without sex and companionship is a small price to pay, given what I did.'

'Thirio,' Lucinda groaned. 'I'm so sorry you feel this way.' She struggled to know what else to say. 'You couldn't have known that would happen.'

'No,' he agreed, voice grim. 'But the way I used to behave, it was only a matter of time.'

She thought about the photos she'd seen of him on the Internet, the lifestyle he used to lead. 'You aren't the only twenty-something who's enjoyed going out and partying, who's then done something stupid because they were drunk, and young.'

'It killed my parents.' His eyes were haunted. 'Would you forgive yourself?'

'Listen to me.' She put her hand on his cheek. 'You have to, for one reason. Your parents would want you to. Do you think your mother and father would wish you to sacrifice your enjoyment in life as some kind of price for their deaths? Of course not. If they loved you at all, and I'm sure they did, they would want you to live your life *for* them. You should be ringing every moment of delight, and feeling it on their behalf. Make your life a tribute, Thirio, not a torment.'

'Beautiful words,' he said, his tone showing that he had heard them without intending to listen. 'But this is how it needs to be. It's the only way I can live with myself.'

Sadness filled her chest. His grief was palpable, so too the tragedy of what had unfolded.

'Would you tell me about them?' she asked, nestling her head back on his wounded chest, knowing now that the outward scars were nothing compared to the marks he carried on the walls of his heart.

His chest rose with his intake of breath, then fell as he expelled slowly, a little unevenly. 'What would you like to know?'

She put her arm over his chest, holding him tight, reassuring him and caring for him. 'Anything you want to tell me.'

And as the dawn sky gradually permitted more

light, Thirio spoke of his parents. He told stories of his childhood vacations, travelling, laughing, having fun. He spoke of his mother's love of Christmas, and how she'd infused that time of year with so much magic, right up until that last year. He spoke about the runs he and his father would go on, miles and miles of silence and then how they'd stop, and talk about nothing in particular. How his dad always made him feel as though he could do anything he wanted, and his mother made him feel as though he wasn't doing enough. He talked about how time had changed his perspective. He used to hate the way his mother hounded him but now he understood how frustrated she must have been by his choices, how desperately she was trying to shake him out of the lifestyle he had chosen. And he spoke of the arguments they'd had, in the last few years, when his life had been off track and he hadn't wanted to go home and listen to his parents.

'After they died, Evie and I inherited everything they owned, equally. Right down the middle. But Evie was still a legal minor, not to gain control of her share of the family's companies for another four years. They were mine to run. I dedicated myself to that. My father had been so devoted to his work, and I'd always neglected that side of our life, not wanting to know anything about the corporate world. I immersed myself in it, so that I could understand and take over.'

'All while you were recovering from your own injuries?' she asked gently, as the sun pierced the forest with a single beam of golden light.

'It was the perfect opportunity. I was bed-bound in hospital for over a month.'

She gasped softly. His injuries must have been very severe.

'When I was released, work became my life. It has been ever since.'

The rest, she knew. Part of her research had told her that Thirio Skartos had taken the already magnificent family fortune and at least trebled it in the last few years. He regularly topped rich lists around the world. But he was also known for his social conscience. His investment in the infrastructure of developing countries had funded schools and highways, and their family foundation had contributed billions of dollars to refugee causes.

'And your charitable work?'

'I donate money.' He brushed it aside.

'You do good, Thirio. A lot of good.'

Silence crackled around them. She yawned, though she wasn't tired. Her mind was wired, even if her body wanted to sleep.

'I do what I think they would want me to. I try to live up to the person they wish I'd been.'

Her heart shattered for him. His pain was so intense.

'"If only" is the most useless phrase in the

world, Thirio.' She stroked his chest tenderly. 'You can't go back in time and follow a different course.'

'I know that.' The words were ripped from him.

'But all the things you've just told me about your parents, that's what you need to think about. Remember how much they loved you, even when they didn't agree with you. Remember how your mother tried to fight to get you to find your potential, and how your father tolerated and supported the phase you were in. They adored you, Thirio. If they were here, they'd put their arms around you and hug you and tell you that it's okay, that they forgive you, and want you to be happy. For them, for Evie, for everyone who's ever cared about you.' Her voice cracked and her own heart gave a little stumble, as feelings she couldn't decipher jumbled through her. Suddenly, her own fate seemed tied to his happiness. This was a temporary union, and yet she couldn't imagine going back to her life and leaving him here, carrying this weight all on his own.

She couldn't imagine leaving him at all.

The sun crested higher, dousing the valley in gold, spreading light across the land just as her heart finally woke up and made itself heard.

Lucinda had sworn she'd never love another person in her life. The fear of rejection was paralysing, and had made it impossible. She'd *chosen* to be alone, without realising that love wasn't really something you had any say in. By spending time with Thirio, she'd opened the door to a world that was inevitable, from the moment they'd met.

She loved him.

But she *couldn't*. She must be mistaken. It was sympathy that was tearing her apart, making her pulse race and her heart thump. It was grief for him, that was all. Once she was back in London, she'd feel differently. Then, everything would be normal.

The cost of loving someone like Thirio would be way too high for Lucinda. She closed her eyes, shutting out the world, Thirio and, most of all, her awakening feelings, simply trusting that things would be different and better when she woke.

After his parents' deaths, he'd been urged to speak to therapists, counsellors, psychologists. He'd been urged to *talk about it*, as though saying how wrong he'd been, over and over, would help at all. He'd never taken that advice. He hadn't wanted to speak to anyone about his complicity in the accident. He hadn't wanted to feel better.

His conversation with Lucinda was a first, and yet, strangely, he didn't regret it. Somehow, it was right that she should know about this part of him. He couldn't explain why, but he suspected it had something to do with the way she looked at him. As though he were perfect.

When he wasn't, and he needed her to know that. He didn't want her to think he was some kind of hero after what he'd done. He didn't deserve the admiration or respect of anyone, let alone a person as wonderful and decent as Lucinda.

He was glad she was leaving today, even when he acknowledged that her departure would be a wrench. In the space of a few short days, he had become used to her presence. He'd liked not being alone. He'd liked knowing she was working in the office he'd made for her. He'd liked walking past and hearing her hum or her fingers clicking over the keyboard.

But it was a fantasy, and now, it was time to get back to reality.

He flicked the coffee machine to life, lining up two cups as he looked out at the same view he'd been staring at for years. There was something about the age of the forest that comforted him. Hundreds of years of growth, these trees had weathered everything, and they'd seen much. Death, destruction, grief, loss. They were the witnesses to humanity's failings, and its successes. His own grief would seem inconsequential to the forest.

But it wasn't to Thirio. Nor was his guilt. Absent-mindedly, he ran his fingers over his chest, feeling the knotted flesh beneath his shirt, the gesture one he did often, reminding himself of his failings.

He needed that reminder particularly this morning, when the pleasures of this weekend threatened to blank out the pain he deserved to feel.

'Good morning.' Lucinda's voice was soft and croaky as she padded into the kitchen behind him. Thirio turned, and his whole body exploded in an unwelcome, automatic response to her appearance. She was so beautiful and so sexy. Her hair was dishevelled about her heart-shaped face, and she wore a shirt of his, long and oversized, only the three middle buttons done up so his eyes dropped to the swell of her cleavage first then the sweep of her shapely legs next. But it wasn't just desire that was making his heart hop and skip. It was the look in her eyes.

As if he were perfect.

Even after what he'd told her.

Even after what he'd done.

He ground his teeth together, instinctively pushing away her kindness and acceptance. He didn't deserve either.

'Coffee?' His tone was brusque and before he turned back to the machine he saw the hurt that lined her eyes and wanted to fix it, to take back the rough question.

'Oh.' The soft sound of disappointment tightened something in his gut. But he told himself he was glad. He wasn't perfect and she needed to understand that. 'Yes, please. What time is it?'

'Eleven.'

'Eleven?' She moaned. 'Why did you let me sleep so late? I have to leave soon.'

And that was why. Coward that he was, Thirio couldn't bear to spend more time with her. Not much more. There was danger in her company, danger in their conversations.

'We were up all night. I presumed you'd be tired.'

'I was,' she agreed. 'But still…'

'Are you comfortable with what you've achieved this weekend?' He pulled the cup away from the machine and turned, handing it to her, watching as she took it. A small frown was on her lips.

'Honestly?' Her eyes searched his, probing, pushing. 'I'm tempted to say no, so you'll invite me back next weekend.'

She was sounding him out, trying to work out what he wanted. Was there more here? Would he offer her more? He couldn't lead her on, no matter how much he wanted to see her again. It wasn't fair to Lucinda. She deserved more than he could ever give.

'If you need to organise anything else, you're welcome to come back. Just let Travis know the details and he'll organise a flight.'

He saw the businesslike words hit their mark. She stood her ground but something in her expression seemed to recoil. Just as he'd wanted, he told himself.

'If this is about last night, Thirio, please don't beat yourself up for talking to me. I'm glad you told me about what happened. I like that you shared that with me.'

His gut twisted. He'd liked it too. But that was the problem. He didn't *want* to like anything about his life.

'We both knew this was a weekend thing. You're leaving in a few hours. What more do you want me to say?'

Even as he spoke the words, he heard them as she must and wanted to take them back. He'd gone too far. They were too cutting. Too cold. Too careless. *So fix it.* But how, and, more importantly, why? She needed to leave and to forget about him. What had started out as a harmless, inevitable fling was now edged with danger, because he knew her better. He knew her softness and vulnerability and he felt a strange yearning to protect her, to keep her safe and make her smile. But these were not skills he had. He couldn't be trusted.

'Nothing.' She sipped her coffee, looking away from him, and he had the terrible, awful feeling that she might be about to cry. But a second later, she faced him, her expression composed. 'I've co-ordinated everything I need.'

It was the answer he wanted to hear, so why did his gut sink like a stone, all the way to the tiled floor at his feet?

'So you won't need to come back again?'

Hurt lashed her features but she sipped her coffee, using those few seconds to hide that pain. 'No.' Her throat muscles bunched. 'I mean, yes, but not until right before the wedding.' She hesitated. 'If that's okay with you?'

He didn't want her to feel as though she had to ask him for permission! He wanted to tell her she was always welcome here, but it was all too hard, too fraught. He closed his eyes, pushing back the doubts he felt, and focusing on the well-worn path he'd chosen. Six years of loneliness were behind him, a lifetime in front.

'Of course. I expected as much when I hired you.'

She flinched, right before she turned away. When she placed the coffee cup down on the bench, it was with too much force, all of the emotions she was containing coming out in the splash of dark liquid that landed on the countertop.

He wanted to apologise. He could taste the word in his mouth, he could feel the explanation forming, but to what end? He had to let her go. A curse had fallen on him the night his parents had died, and he couldn't draw Lucinda into it. He couldn't let her get any closer. He couldn't let her care for him, maybe even love him. He couldn't let her put her life in his hands. How could he live with himself if he made another mistake and she paid the price?

He had to let her go.

And so he did exactly that, watching her retreating back without moving, even when every cell in his body demanded that he follow.

CHAPTER THIRTEEN

EVEN AFTER THEIR DEATHS, he hadn't wallowed. Thirio had been full of purpose. He had focused on the businesses, on learning everything he could about his parents' work, and then, he'd thrown himself into being alone. Isolated. Sober, so that he could feel every single thread of remorse and guilt and responsibility, so that he could hate himself without the softening effects of alcohol. He had avoided the phone calls of his friends until they'd stopped calling, giving up on him completely.

But he hadn't wallowed.

Even his guilt had been directed and ambitious—he had given himself a lifelong sentence and set about observing it.

But this was different.

Lucinda was everywhere in the castle, even when she was, now, nowhere. He felt her here, most of all, in the room they'd first made love in. His fingertips brushed her bed and memories jerked through him. He walked past her office and heard her fingertips on the keyboard, but when he looked inside, the computer was abandoned, the space empty. Her fragrance, just a hint, lingered, so he stepped inside, breathing in deeply. She was in his bed, in his shower, on the terrace, in the kitchen. Her hands were on his coffee cup, his chest, his scar, his face. Her lips, oh, her lips. He felt them everywhere, memories cutting through him, heating him and destroying him even as they gave him a strength he hadn't known for a long time. Something bright caught his eye and he bent down, digging his finger into the gap between the floorboards, feeling something sharp. Frowning, he pushed at it harder, loosening it, pulling it free as a thousand memories exploded through him. Clutching it in his hand, he closed his eyes, remembering this, her, everything.

The world had shifted. Something fundamental was changing, but he fought that. He'd known he was playing with fire. He'd tried to resist her. He *had* resisted her, for as long as he could, but in the end, it was impossible. Yet even as he'd succumbed, he'd known it would have to end, and now she was gone. This was just something he'd have to deal with.

Still, the wedding loomed, not for the event it was, not for the fact it was his sister's day, but because it would bring Lucinda back to the *castile*— for the last time. He would need to be strong and he would need to remember: nothing good came from wanting what you could never have.

Anxiety was a tangle in the pit of her stomach. After all her hard work—and the last two weeks had involved twenty-hour days, hours of conference calls, flights to meet contractors, making contingency plans for any event, any unforeseeable crisis—and finally, she knew, beyond a shadow of a doubt, that everything was in place. This wedding was going to be spectacular—so much as she could control—and Evie was going to have the time of her life.

And Thirio?

How was he feeling about the impending arrival of one hundred and fifty of Europe's elite at his hideaway castle?

If she'd known then what she knew now, would she have pushed this plan on him? Would she even have dared suggest it? The castle was his sanctuary, and he deserved that. But didn't he also deserve to be made to face reality again? Did Evie know how shattered he was by their parents' deaths? Did Evie understand why he hid himself away?

So many questions had clouded Lucinda's mind since leaving the *castile,* but she had reconciled herself to the fact she would never have these answers. It wasn't her place to know.

Thirio had made that abundantly clear.

Even his name sent a shiver of anticipation down her spine, but she quelled it. An expert at concealing her feelings, Lucinda knew, nonetheless, that this weekend would test her as no other time in her life ever had.

As the plane lifted off the tarmac, she forced herself to focus on the acquisition of the company—being handled through a third-party broker. She didn't want her stepmother knowing that she was behind the purchase until the ink was dried on the contracts. Despite the amount of money she'd offered, she worried that Elodie would refuse to sell, just to be unkind to Lucinda. Again.

But so far, everything looked in order. Lucinda was going to get everything she'd worked so hard for. She should have been delirious. But where she'd expected joy and contentment to finally fill her heart, there was only a dull, throbbing ache of emptiness. Somehow, her dreams had shifted, and her father's business was no longer the pinnacle of what she wanted in life…

He had intended to install Lucinda in the staff quarters, with the caterers and housekeepers who'd been brought to the *castile* to manage the logistics of the weekend. Over eighty workers filling a dormitory-style wing of the castle, just as they had in the past, when the family had travelled here for Christmas vacations and his parents had put on lavish parties that had drawn half of Europe—or so it had felt to a young Thirio. But as the wedding approached, he'd found himself giving instructions for the room she'd occupied on her first night at the *castile* to be made available for her. It was close to his. A test, if ever he'd known one. But it was a test he intended to pass.

And yet, he also wanted to be near her. To see her smile. To help her if she needed it. He was no one's knight in shining armour but that didn't mean he didn't care about Lucinda. He wanted this weekend to be perfect. For Evie, but also for Lucinda, who had so much riding on it.

And he wanted to see her, as much as he could. Even from a distance. He just needed…to look.

Would that really be enough?

She refused to take it as an omen that her luggage was lost on the flight. If anything, Lucinda convinced herself that that was her little piece of bad luck for the weekend, already got out of the way. Now, there would only be good luck! Besides, the luggage would turn up within a day or so, the airline had promised.

Closing her mind off to the suggestion that it was a bad omen, she stepped out of her hire car with a look of assumed calm. She wasn't going to think about Thirio. She wasn't going to wonder if he was watching. But, just in case he was, she wasn't going to let him see how shredded her nerves were!

She walked to the front door with head held high, smiling when it was drawn inwards by a housekeeper in a black dress and pale grey apron.

'Good morning,' the woman said with an efficient nod. 'Miss Villeneuve?'

'Yes.' She held out her hand in greeting.

The older woman with her golden hair pulled back into a bun extended her own hand. 'I'm Vera. Come this way. Do you have a bag?'

Lucinda recounted the story as they walked, noting with pleasure how many of her instructions had already been implemented. The florists had been busy, and arrangements of bright flowers stood all through the common areas, huge bunches that were fragrant and meaningful— the national flower of Nalvania was the star of the group, with its pale pink and yellow blooms dominating the centre—surrounded by peace lilies and laurel leaves to represent Greece. There were also pale pink hydrangeas—believed to bring luck—peonies for prosperity and long tendrils of rosemary for remembrance. Each arrangement perfectly matched the illustrations Lucinda had sent. She paused to inhale one as they passed, tears touching her eyes.

Evie was going to love it.

She was so caught up in the details that she didn't notice Vera leading her up a very familiar set of stairs, past a window that had been broken four weeks earlier and which was now perfectly restored, so that no one except her and Thirio would know that a tree had crashed right through it.

But when Vera led Lucinda to the door of the room she'd been sleeping in that night, her heart leaped into her throat and her feet refused to move.

'There must be some mistake,' she said with a small shake of her head. 'I'm to stay in the staff quarters.'

'There is no bed available,' Vera said apologetically. 'Mr Skartos suggested this room instead.'

Lucinda's lips parted in consternation. The last thing she wanted was to be difficult, but she'd purposefully placed herself with the staff, to avoid any blurring of lines between herself and Thirio. Whatever they'd shared was over. She was just someone who worked for him now.

'It doesn't seem appropriate.' She clutched at straws. 'Is there nowhere else?'

Vera's laugh was soft and kind. 'The castle will be overflowing with guests, Miss Villeneuve. Every room is spoken for.'

Resignation hit Lucinda between the shoulder blades.

As Vera began to walk away, Lucinda spun on her heel. 'Will you let me know when my suitcase turns up?'

She asked the question at the exact moment

Thirio prowled from his room, head bent, hands in pockets. She knew then that he hadn't been watching for her, because he looked genuinely surprised to see her. Almost as if he hadn't remembered she was coming a day ahead of the ceremony.

'Lucinda.' His voice was deep, wrapping around Lucinda's whole body, drawing her towards him even when her feet stayed firmly planted on the ground.

'Thirio.' She dipped her head in a polite greeting.

'Did your suitcase get lost?'

Vera smiled curtly and left.

'The airline lost it.' Lucinda's words were clipped. She looked towards her bedroom door. 'I didn't intend to sleep here. The staff quarters would have been fine.'

'They get draughty.'

She tried not to let it warm her heart to think that he had made this choice out of concern for her comfort. She stared at him, completely off kilter. It was as though they were strangers, and yet they weren't. She *knew* him. Not in an encyclopaedic way, where she could quote every single fact about his life, but in a true and meaningful way. She knew what made him tick. She knew what mattered to him. And most of all, she knew what he was afraid of and excited for. And more than that, she loved him.

Pain lanced her as she forced herself to fully

face the truth for the first time, to stare down the hopelessness of loving him, knowing he would not—could not—love her back.

'Excuse me,' she said with quiet resignation. 'I'm going to freshen up before I check in with the caterers.'

'Have dinner with me tonight.'

It was not a question. But nor was it at all expected. Heat rushed into her cheeks. She forced herself to meet his eyes, as her stomach rolled and flipped and tightened with uncertainty.

'I don't think that's a good idea.' *Have dinner with him,* her heart pleaded. Regardless of the damage that would be done to that very organ, she didn't want to take the safe road. She wanted as much of Thirio as he was willing to give to her, even while acknowledging that it would never be enough.

'Perhaps not.' He drew closer, his eyes probing hers. 'Do it anyway.'

Wasn't that just what her heart had said?

She stared up at him, lost, destroyed, hopelessly wanting. She breathed in, searching for words, and tasted him in her mouth. Her knees went weak. 'Thirio—'

'It's just dinner.' But he lifted a hand and caught her cheek, touching her as though he couldn't bear not to.

'Is it?' she pushed, forcing him to be honest.

His lips curled in a derisive smile. 'No.'

'Then what is it?' She was surprised by the bold question, but she was also glad she'd asked it.

'One more night,' he said simply.

'And then what?'

He frowned. 'And then you go away again.'

'For ever?'

A muscle jerked low in his jaw. His nod was slow. A surrender to the necessity of that. But was it really necessary?

'It has to be that way.'

'Why?'

'You know the answer to that.'

She did. At least, she knew what he believed. But he was wrong. How could she make him see that? And how could she possibly fight for him to understand?

He would say no.

He would reject her.

Thirio would become just another person in her life who didn't care for her. Someone else she loved who wouldn't love her back. Just like after her father had died and she'd turned to her step-mother and stepsisters, expecting consolation and receiving cruelty. Just like when she'd fallen in love with Beckett and he'd chosen her stepsister.

Thirio would be just the same. He would choose not to be with her.

And she couldn't bear it.

How could she fight when the outcome was already ordained?

Perhaps this would be all they'd ever have. Snatches of time with no hope for a future.

Sadness cloyed at her throat. She wished she could refuse him. She wished she could tell him to go to hell. But she loved him, and she would take whatever time they had, before the real end game.

'Dinner,' she agreed finally, her voice uneven.

His relief was obvious, but so too his concern. This wasn't easy for either of them.

He had planned to avoid her. Simply to know she was here and be near her without touching, without speaking more than was necessary. But as soon as he'd seen her, the plan had crumbled around him and he'd reached for her as a drowning man would a lifeline. He'd clutched at more time together. More of Lucinda.

It ran contrary to everything he'd planned.

He actually felt nervous. Thirio Skartos! A man who'd dated hundreds of women in his life felt as though his legs were going to fall out from under him as he waited for Lucinda. The only advantage to having his castle overrun by staff was that he'd been able to have the terrace set up like a restaurant. One single table stood in the middle of the space, covered in a white cloth with a candle at its centre. Strings of fairy lights ran overhead, and soft jazz music played through the speakers. The air was heavy with the scent of food covered with sterling silver lids. Brightly coloured cushions had been scattered on the far side of the terrace, as well as a picnic rug. It looked perfect.

Too perfect.

It looked like a night of promise, but this was no such thing. There was nothing Thirio could offer Lucinda. Would she mind? Would she hate him? He almost hoped she would.

'Wow.' The word curled around him, so he closed his eyes before turning, needing to rally his strength before he saw her.

He spun slowly, bracing himself, but there was nothing he could do to stop the wave of awareness that cascaded through him.

She was beautiful.

More beautiful than she'd ever looked.

It was ridiculous. She was wearing the same thing she'd been wearing earlier, but her long hair was out now, loose down her back and tumbling over her shoulders, and her feet were bare. That small detail sent his nerves into overdrive. It was so intimate. So...at home.

The phrase gripped him like a noose.

This was his home; not hers.

'Please.' He cleared his throat, gesturing to the table. She walked towards it without sitting down. Her fingers shook visibly as she reached for the bottle of red wine and poured herself a glass, then moved around the table and poured him one. Her fingers were still shaking when she picked both up and walked slowly, purposefully towards him, extending a glass. He reached to take it, his fingers closing over hers without regret. The contact seared his skin, sending arrows of awareness darting through him.

'You hurt me.'

The raw admission was like a punch in the gut. She pulled her hand free at the same time she took a gulp of her wine, eyes fixing on the view, the silhouette of hundreds of pine trees against the dark night sky.

He didn't ask what she meant. He knew the answer.

'I was abrupt,' he admitted. 'I hadn't expected things to go so far between us.'

'I know that.' She nodded softly, her kindness the last thing he wanted and deserved.

'I thought it was just physical. I thought we could sleep together and then I'd be able to move on. I didn't know you'd get under my skin, Lucinda.'

She flinched a little. 'And you don't want me there?'

'I don't want you to care for me,' he said automatically. 'I don't want you to hope that you can change me, and what I want in life.'

'Which is to be alone.'

'Yes.' He stared at her, to convince her, even when doubts were flicking through him.

'What if I want to help you feel better?'

He shunned that. 'I don't deserve it.'

'Says who?'

'Anyone who can see clearly.'

'An eye for an eye? Is that it?'

He took a drink of his wine, barely appreciating the excellence. 'Something like that.'

'What about what's right for Evie? What about what's right for me? What about the people who care about you, who want you to be happy? Don't we deserve some consideration?'

Ice flooded Thirio. 'I've been honest with you from the start about my…limitations.'

'But you weren't honest,' she countered angrily. 'You told me you wanted to be alone and yet you reached for me with both hands. You do it every time we're together.' He ground his teeth. 'But you didn't tell me why you were fighting this, until it was too late. If you had, I would have known that you'd made the decision from a place of fear.'

'You can't possibly understand.'

'Maybe not.' She sighed. 'All I know is that you're denying us both something really great because you're living in the past.'

'Only it's not my past,' he ground out. 'It's my present, my future, my waking nightmare. Every time I look in the mirror I see the evidence of what I did. You're asking me to forget—'

'Not to forget. But to forgive yourself.'

'And I'm telling you, I can't. I never will.'

'Even for me?'

'I don't deserve—' He shook his head. 'This

has no future.' He forced the words to ring with certainty. 'I don't know how else I can say it to make you believe…'

'Tell me you don't want me,' she said quietly, stoicism in the words.

He tried to shape the words, but couldn't. 'I want you to forget me after the wedding. I should have been strong enough to end this before it started.'

Sadness washed over Lucinda's face, but her lips twisted into a smile that was ghostly, bittersweet. 'I'll always be glad you didn't.' She angled her face away for a moment, drawing in a shuddering breath. 'Let's eat, Thirio. Tomorrow's a big day. We both need a good night's sleep.'

Regret clawed through him. He wanted—with all his heart—things he could never have. But that didn't stop him wanting.

CHAPTER FOURTEEN

AFTER HER FATHER had died, Lucinda had learned a lot about the circles of control. There were some things in her life she could control, and into those things, she poured her energy. The circles that were beyond her ability of influence, she had to make her peace with.

Her suitcase not arriving was beyond her control.

The weather too.

So when she woke and saw the hint of storm clouds on the horizon, she didn't put her energy into worrying about them. She'd planned for this. There were wet-weather contingencies for miles. She pushed out of bed, trying not to think about the fact Thirio was just across the hallway as she moved to the window. Despite the fact it was still early, an army of staff was positioning canopy tents to form a walkway from the makeshift car park to the entrance of the castle. There were also, she noted with pleasure, dozens of umbrellas in a basket, by the door. The umbrellas had been printed with Evie and Erik's monogram, and the date of their wedding—a keepsake for guests, albeit a practical one.

As she'd predicted, the day was busy. There were checklists upon checklists and, despite the fact the contractors worked like a well-oiled machine, Lucinda was kept so busy overseeing the preparations that she could only devote about half of her brain power to Thirio, and wondering where he was. Wondering *how* he was. Opening his doors to hundreds of people was Thirio's idea of hell, and yet he'd done it, out of love for his sister. And guilt too? Because he blamed himself for their parents' deaths?

She pushed the thought away. It was crippling in its intensity, so too her desire to run to him and kiss him until that guilt ceased to exist. She hated that he felt that way. Their deaths were a curse from which he would never escape.

But what if love was the answer? What if love would break that curse?

She stopped what she was doing, causing the housekeeper to look at her with concern. Lucinda stared straight ahead, her heart thumping hard against her ribs. What if she told him? And suddenly, it wasn't a question of whether or not she would, but *when* she could. The knowledge that she loved him was like an oppressive weight, and only revealing it to him would lighten that.

Doubtless, he would reject her, but that didn't

change the fact that she wanted him to know how she felt. She needed him to understand that she saw him as he was, she knew about his past, about the act for which he hated himself, and she loved him regardless. She needed him to understand that she loved him enough for both of them. And if he rejected her, it would hurt, but at least he would know that he was worth loving.

She continued with her work, her brain now almost fully engaged in thinking about Thirio, until about an hour before the wedding, when one of the Nalvanian palace staff came up to her.

'Excuse me, madam, but Miss Skartos is asking for you.'

'Is there a problem?'

'No. She's this way.'

Lucinda followed behind as the servant led her to the old family quarters. Thirio had gestured to it without entering and Lucinda understood now. This part of the palace was alive with his childhood. Photographs hung on the wall of a young Thirio, his parents, his sister. She paused, looking at one with eyes that were misted over. Any doubts she had flew from her mind.

She loved him, and he had to know that. He'd lost so much when his parents had died and instead of allowing himself to grieve, he'd thrown himself into his guilt instead.

When Lucinda entered Evie's room, she gasped. 'You look so beautiful.' Evie was a picture of elegance and glamour, in a white silk dress with a pale blue sash crossed diagonally over one shoulder. Her blonde hair had been secured into a bun and a diamond tiara sat atop her head.

'Thank you.' Her smile was loaded with pleasure. 'I'm so excited.'

'That's exactly how a bride should feel.' Lucinda nodded encouragingly. 'Everything is organised. Can I get you something while you're waiting? Tea? Something to eat?'

'No, I actually have something for you.'

'Oh?'

'Follow me.' Evie smiled serenely as she sashayed across the room, to a walk-in wardrobe. It was only a quarter full, with the clothes Evie had brought for the wedding. But at the end, there was the most stunning dress Lucinda had ever seen. Silver, with wide straps and a sweetheart neckline, and a structured skirt that fell to the ground. There were tiny diamantés all over the bodice, so that it gave the impression of sparkling, just like the fresh snow on treetops.

'That's stunning.'

'I'm glad you think so. I got it out for you to wear.'

Lucinda's eyes were enormous when she turned to face Evie. 'For *me*?'

'I understand your suitcase went missing, and I won't hear any of this business about you not attending. You should get to come and enjoy your handiwork.'

'That's not really how this works,' Lucinda insisted.

'Please? I don't know why, but I really feel like you should come. Think of it as a wedding present.'

Lucinda stared at her client, the woman she'd sworn she'd move mountains to give the perfect wedding day to. 'It really is a beautiful dress.'

'It was my mother's,' Evie said quietly, moving towards it. 'She had the most incredible taste. Her wardrobe is classic.'

'I can't possibly wear it.' Lucinda was stricken.

'Nonsense.'

Lucinda moved closer to the dress, running her fingers over the bodice. 'So many diamantés,' she said with appreciation for how they were stitched into the fabric.

'They're not diamantés.'

Leaning closer, Lucinda, heart pounding, realised that Evie was right. The bodice was covered in tiny diamonds—and some not so tiny. 'Evie, this dress is...'

'Please.' Evie waved a hand through the air. 'It will be perfect on you. Let me help you get ready.'

'I—'

'You asked me if I needed anything earlier? It's this. I want to pass the time. Would you oblige me?'

How could Lucinda say no? As she stepped into the dress, then sat while Evie styled her hair into a crown of braids, Lucinda felt as though *she* were the princess, going to the ball, and Evie her fairy godmother. Thirio was right, though. He wasn't Prince Charming. But did it follow that they couldn't have their own Happily Ever After?

Thirio—along with every red-blooded male in the marquee—saw her enter and watched as she moved gracefully towards an empty seat and slid into it, eyes forward. Not looking around. Not looking for him.

But he couldn't look away.

Lucinda was always stunning. He'd seen her in many guises now, and he found her beautiful no matter what she was wearing. But in this dress, she was some kind of untouchable fantasy, her swan-like neck on display courtesy of the hair-style.

'She looks lovely, doesn't she?'

He turned as his sister joined him, and a lump formed in his throat. Because Evie was so beautiful, so like their parents, and he loved her so damned much. He put his arms around her, aching for the fact they weren't here, aching for what he'd taken from Evie, but also feeling gladness that he could give her this day, this wedding, at the *castile*. Lucinda had been right about how much this would mean and he was glad he'd listened.

'You look lovely,' he corrected.

'Thank you.' She pulled away, blinking back tears. 'Don't make me cry.'

'What did I say?'

'You didn't say anything. It's the expression on your face.' She pressed a kiss to his cheek. 'I love you, Thirio.'

He squeezed her hand rather than saying it back. The words jammed inside him.

'Are you ready?'

'I was ready three years ago.'

'You met Erik three years ago,' he pointed out.

'And I've known ever since then.' She smiled up at him, the certainty in her features shifting something in his chest. She loved her fiancé. She knew beyond a shadow of a doubt. He didn't analyse that thought any further.

The ceremony was long, repeated in Nalvanian after the English vows, but he focused on the bride and groom the entire time, standing with them, only letting his eyes stray twice to where Lucinda sat, her eyes fixed on Evie, a soft, contemplative smile on her face.

He felt as if he'd been punched in the gut.

'Would you dance with me?'

It was late into the night. Everything had gone perfectly. Lucinda was glowing. And when Thirio approached her, asking her to dance, she spun, her heart thumping, certainty forming a shield of courage.

'Absolutely.'

His eyes held hers as he took her hand, then turned and led her onto the dance floor, drawing her close to his chest, holding her against him as they began to move, slowly.

'Everything went well,' he said after a moment, the compliment weaving through her.

'Yes.'

'When will you fly back?'

Her heart twisted painfully. The prospect of leaving—and for good—filled her mouth with acid.

'Tomorrow.' She pulled back a little to see how he reacted, but his face was angled away. Was she imagining a stiffening of his frame?

'And you'll buy the company?'

'It's already in motion,' she agreed with a nod, wondering why that now left her with an empty feeling in the pit of her stomach. It was as though she was putting down firm roots, but in the wrong place.

'I'm glad. You deserve that.'

He was wrong. She deserved so much more. She deserved to be loved as she loved. She deserved what she'd been denied for years. She hadn't always thought so. Before meeting Thirio, she'd believed the answer was to bury herself away from the possibility of love, not to take a gamble lest she got hurt. But Thirio had changed her. She realised now that love was worth fighting for. Even when there was a risk of loss, rejection and pain.

'Can we go somewhere a little more private?' she asked, putting a hand to his chest and drawing his attention.

His reluctance was obvious, but so too his yearning. He was afraid of what he felt. He was afraid of what they shared. He was afraid he wouldn't be able to say 'no' to her. 'Please.'

His eyes closed and he nodded, a muscle jerking in his jaw. 'Come with me.' He laced their fingers together and pulled her with him towards the entrance of the ballroom, then through the wide doors, past the candelabras that were weaved with long strands of ivy, then out onto a terrace, this one far enough away from the revellers that they could only hear the strains of the music.

'Private enough?' he asked, warily.

'Yes.' She had to do this. A thousand nerves fired through her but she didn't change course. 'I will leave tomorrow, if that's really what you want,' she said. 'And I will never contact you again. You made a choice six years ago to live your life alone, to pay for what you see as your crime.' Sadness washed over her. 'But I would stay if you asked me.'

His eyes flared wide.

'I would stay, and I would live here with you, a part of you, just like you're a part of me.'

His lips parted.

'I love you.' She said it simply, in the end, because her love for him was simple. Brick by brick, it had been placed inside her heart, and it would always be there.

He groaned, catching her face in his hands, holding her steady. 'Don't say that.'

She felt the ping of hurt. She'd expected his rejection, and thought she'd protected herself against it, but she was wrong. It stung. She blinked quickly.

'I love you, with all my heart,' she pushed on regardless. 'You are worthy of that love. You are deserving of it. And more than that, you are deserving of happiness. I want to be with you. I want to love you. I want to be loved by you. All you have to do is open yourself up to that future. Step away from the darkness, Thirio.'

'It's not that simple. The darkness is inside me.' He pressed a palm to his chest. 'I can't escape it.'

'You can choose happiness.' She lifted up onto the tips of her toes and brushed her lips to his. 'You can choose me.'

'No.'

She ignored his rejection. 'You will always feel that pain. You will always feel grief and guilt and regret. But you can feel other emotions alongside it. Your life can be a tribute to your parents, the sort of life they'd want you to lead.'

'No,' he said again, but she understood: he was

rejecting her because he was scared. He wanted her to leave, only that wouldn't solve anything for either of them.

'Whenever we get close, you push me away,' she said gently. 'Does it ever really work?'

He stared at her without speaking.

'Do you ever actually forget about me?'

His jaw shifted, teeth clenching.

'I didn't think so,' she said softly, reaching for her throat, for the necklace she always wore. Except she'd lost it, weeks ago. Instead, she tapped her finger to her pulse, hoping for calm.

'What is your point?' he asked after a moment.

'Fighting this is futile. You won't win. I love you, and I'm almost certain you love me too. You're going to be miserable if you let me go.'

His lips tightened into something like a grimace. 'I'm used to that.'

She shook her head sadly. 'So you're going to use what you feel to punish yourself some more? Denying us both what we want in life because you're so hell-bent on this prison sentence you've created?'

'I told you from the beginning—'

'But everything's changed since then! Hasn't it?'

He stared at her for several beats.

'Answer me.'

He expelled a rough sigh. 'Some things have changed. Some things haven't. I can't click my fingers and alter my past. I can't change the fabric of who I am.'

'I'm not asking you to.'

'Yes. You are.' He ground out the words with frustration. 'You don't get it. I don't want to be loved. I don't want anyone to love me, to trust me, to put their faith in me.'

'Because you think you don't deserve that? Or because you're worried you'll do something that will hurt me?'

'I killed my parents, Lucinda.'

'It was an accident.' She lifted up and kissed him again. 'An accident.' She whispered the words against the corner of his mouth. 'An awful, tragic, unforgettable loss, but an accident nonetheless. I can't promise you that I'll never get hurt or sick or even die. I know better than anyone how cruel and unpredictable life can be. But I do know I'd rather live every day I possibly can with you. My heart is full of love for you—it always will be— whether I'm here or in England or anywhere in the world.' She breathed in deeply. 'I know you're angry. You have every right to be. You lost so much that night, and you haven't let yourself feel that loss. Guilt is different from grief. Perhaps it's better for you to feel guilt as there's an element of control in it, I don't know.'

'Psychoanalysing me doesn't change a thing,' he said gruffly.

'Perhaps not.' Her smile was a bitter twist of

her lips. 'Only, I wasn't sure if you knew what you were doing. You think staying here, hiding out from the world, is penance? It's cowardly. You're giving in to guilt, rather than facing your grief. You're hiding from it, instead of learning to walk alongside it. You will miss them every day of your life, but you still deserve to have a life.'

He stared down at her, his expression unmoving. Sadness welled inside her. She'd known this would be his response.

'I needed you to know how I feel. Before I met you, I was afraid too, Thirio. I was scared of love and loss. I was hiding as well. I avoided friendships and relationships, any closeness that might lead to me being hurt, and I don't want to live like that any more. You've woken me up and now that I've seen the beauty of closeness, I want to feel it every day. Even when it makes me achingly vulnerable.' Her lips twisted to one side. 'Even when I know that walking away from you will be the hardest thing I've ever done.'

'God, Lucinda. I didn't ask for this!'

She blinked up at him. 'Neither of us did, yet here we are. The question is, what are you going to do about it?'

He stared at her for so long, she thought he wasn't going to answer. And then, slowly, his voice rumbled between them. 'You're wrong. I grieved. I was saturated by it for a long time, and, out of that grief, I made a decision that I could live with. I made a choice to sacrifice certain things to fix what I'd broken.'

'But how does it fix it?' As she asked the question a blade of lightning cut through the night sky, illuminating his face in shadow.

'It means I can live with what I did.'

'By hating yourself?'

'Yes.'

'You deserve so much better, Thirio. Your parents would want—'

'You don't know them.'

'I know what you've told me. I know what I saw in the photos near your sister's room. I know Evie, and how she loves you. I know that you are a good, kind, decent man. And I know that I love you.' She stared at him, willing him to believe her, to say it back. There was only the distant grinding of thunder. 'But I also know how stubborn you are. If this is truly what you want, I'll leave.'

She waited, nerves stretched to breaking point.

'You'll never hear from me again,' she promised, saying the words to herself as much as to Thirio.

'I'm sorry.' The words were a tortured admission that this pain weighed heavily on him.

'Don't apologise to me,' she said with a tilt of her chin. 'This hurts like hell right now, but I'm a better person because of what we shared. You changed me in the best possible way. You drew me into the light, Thirio. I just wish I could have done the same for you.' Her heart cracked into a thousand pieces. 'Please, never forget that I love you. Whenever you are here, alone, ruminating on the past, know that there's someone out there who's seen the parts of you you're ashamed of, and loves you with all her heart.'

She turned and walked away, head held high, managing to keep her tears at bay until she was alone in her room. Only then did she give in to them, and face the reality of the life she would be returning to. A life without Thirio.

CHAPTER FIFTEEN

IT RAINED THAT NIGHT.

All night.

Thirio watched it fall from his bedroom window. He stared out at the rain and forced himself to remember another night, a clear, sunny night, dry and hot, when his arrogance had forced him to fight with his mother, and his selfishness had pushed him out of the door.

He remembered the smell of smoke and the taste of ash. He remembered the sound of death and the knowledge of fault. But as the rain fell, and his heart groaned under the burden of his memories, he felt something else.

Doubt.

Doubt about this path he'd chosen. Doubt about the wisdom of spending his life like this, in his parents' names. Lucinda had said they wouldn't want this for him, and, alone in his room, he admitted to himself that she was right. His parents would have wanted him to forgive himself, and move on.

More than that, for the first time in six years, he allowed himself a fantasy he'd never dared indulge: he wondered if they'd have been proud of him, and the man he'd become. Would his father admire the work Thirio had done with the company, and for their favoured charities? Was he the version of himself his mother had longed to see? Would she smile now to know how different he was? Or would she judge him for making more decisions she didn't agree with, for pushing away Lucinda?

He had reconciled himself to the fact that this was temporary, and yet, as the sky lightened and the moment of her departure approached, he doubted everything.

Most of all, he regretted words he hadn't said, words she deserved to hear. She'd overcome her fears to tell him how she felt—didn't he owe her the same? Regardless of what the future held, shouldn't he show the same courage she'd demonstrated?

It rained all night and he watched every drop, until the sky was wrung dry, and only then did he breathe in deeply and turn, walking towards her before he could change his mind. Walking towards her because, in the end, it was the only thing he could do.

Her bedroom was empty.

Panic laced his veins.

He'd left it too late. His rejection had been too final. She'd left.

He swore into her room, true desperation flooding him. As a weak dawn light filtered into her bedroom, he felt with clarity what he'd lost, and this time, it was the hardest loss he'd ever known. Because it wasn't a drunken mistake. He'd pushed her away. Again and again and again, when she'd been brave enough to face up to what they shared, he'd shut her down, building a wall around himself, fighting for this solitary existence.

He dropped his head, his breathing ragged, the reality of his choices burning through him.

'Thirio?' Her voice was soft, edged with worry. 'Are you okay?'

'Lucinda.' His eyes pierced her. 'You're still here.'

She stepped out of the en suite bathroom, wearing a T-shirt and briefs. He barely noticed her state of undress. He could only stare at her face, her beautiful face, so grateful to see it again when seconds ago he'd been sure she was gone for good, just as he'd asked her to be. 'What did you think?'

It felt foolish now. After all, the logistics of leaving the *castile* in the dead of night, particularly a stormy night, were almost insurmountable.

'That you'd left,' he said with a small shrug of his shoulders.

'Not yet, but soon.'

He hadn't come here to hide from the truth any more. He needed to face up to this. No more delays. 'I don't want you to leave.'

The words filled the room, expanding and contracting until they occupied every space. She stared at him, her features giving nothing away.

'I see.' She hesitated. 'No, actually, I don't. What exactly do you mean?'

Good point. He hadn't exactly made himself clear. 'I knew the moment I met you that you were dangerous to me. You were different and perceptive and kind, and you didn't let me get away with anything. You challenged me from the moment you got here, and I needed that. I needed you.' He still wasn't getting this across. He reached into the pocket of his trousers, withdrawing the small jewel he'd found.

He carried it towards her, his hand closed into a fist until he reached her, then he flatted his palm to reveal what he held.

'Where did you find this?' She reached for the diamond necklace, touching the stone gently, then moving to his palm, pressing a finger to his flesh and closing her eyes.

He did the same, inhaling, tasting her on the tip of his tongue. He pulled away, watching her as he unfastened the chain. 'After you left, I spent a lot of time in your room. No matter what I was doing in the day, I was drawn to that space, as though by being there I could be close to you. I found it in a gap in the floorboards.'

'Oh.'

He lifted it, placing it around her neck, moving behind her so he could fasten it.

'It was my mother's. It's all I have of hers. It means so much to me.'

'I should have returned it before now,' he admitted. 'But I held onto it, because it was a part of you, and I liked having something of yours near me. I knew I was addicted to you, but I thought I could conquer that.'

'I see.' Her voice was soft.

'You have lost so much, and yet you offered me your love. I can't let you go without telling you how I feel.'

Silence cracked, heavy with expectation, but also anxiety. Thirio knew this was a watershed moment, and, after six years of walling himself away, it took concerted effort to step over this threshold. But for Lucinda, for the life his parents would have wanted him to grab, he knew what he had to do.

'You are not just under my skin, *agape mou*, but you are a part of my soul, the owner of my heart—lock and key. You are the other part of me, a part that I have been missing all my life, a part that I hunted for before the accident, and that I have badly needed ever since. I did not think I was broken. If anything, I thought my

decision to remain here was a mark of strength.'
What a fool he'd been!

'But I was wrong. I was shattered by what
happened—splintered into a thousand pieces—
but meeting you—loving you—has made me
whole again. I love you,' he said, simply. 'And
it is a love that has given me the strength I need
to face the world, regardless of what I did. You
were right when you said I must learn to walk
alongside my grief. And I will. But I would
much rather do that with you at my side.'

Her back was to him, but he felt her shoulders
tremble and spun her gently in his arms.

'I love you,' he said again, his eyes showing
the truth of his heart. 'I am yours, Lucinda, in
every way, for all time. I can never thank you
adequately for being brave enough to admit how
you felt, even when I gave you no reason to
think I would welcome your admission.'

'You gave me every reason,' she denied tenderly. 'You love me. I could feel it. I knew it.
And I hoped, more than I have ever hoped for
anything in my life, that you would know it too,
one day. I was willing to wait for you, Thirio,
but I'm so glad I don't have to.'

His laugh was a deep rumble. 'No. No more
waiting.' He pressed his forehead to hers. 'Do
you think the priest could be persuaded to per-
form another ceremony today?' he asked, only
half joking.

She smiled against his lips. 'Sadly, no. There's paperwork required. But perhaps he'll come back in a month?'

Thirio blinked. 'Are you—do you actually mean—?'

She laughed. 'That depends. Were you seriously asking?'

'Lucinda Villeneuve, I want, more than any person has ever wanted anything on this earth, to spend the rest of my life with you. I want to wake up with you, to kiss you, to taste you, to make you smile and to see all your dreams come true. I want to love you as you deserve to be loved, to worship you, to support you and hold you, for as long as we both shall live. You are my other half,' he said simply. 'Will you marry me?'

She nodded. 'In a heartbeat.'

And their hearts *would* beat, both perfectly in synch, for as long as they lived.

Three years later

'Are you absolutely sure about this?' Thirio scanned the paperwork, before passing it to Lucinda.

'One hundred per cent. It's been an amazing ride, but I've achieved what I wanted. Besides, the purchase price is too good to refuse,' she joked, because Mrs Thirio Skartos hardly needed any more money. For this reason, she'd decided to donate the proceeds from the sale of her father's company—which she'd spent three years building into an events powerhouse, with Thirio's support—to a bereavement support charity.

'I know the business will be in safe hands,' she added. 'Much safer than it was before. Reflecting on things, that's what I really wanted. It wasn't that I needed to follow in my father's steps, it was just to stop my stepmother from destroying his legacy.'

'And you have done that, ten times over,' he said with satisfaction, thrilled that the grasping, unkind Elodie and her equally displeasing daughters had disappeared completely from Lucinda's life. Whatever thoughts Elodie had entertained of their marriage being a pathway to billionaire husbands for Sofia and Carina had been swiftly shut down by Thirio, who wasted no time confronting Elodie with his feelings about her cruelty, and telling her she would never be welcome in their home.

Perhaps he'd gone too far, but there was nothing he wouldn't do for his wife. Besides, they had each other, and they had Evie and Erik and their twins, and a small, loyal group of friends that made them feel blessed every day.

'So long as you know I would have supported you working at this company for as long as you wanted.'

'I know that.' She grinned across at him. 'You've been wonderful. But I have something else I'd like to work on now, and I think it's going to take a lot more of my time and energy than rebuilding Dad's business.'

'Oh?' He watched his wife with sheer admiration. Anything she decided to take on, she could accomplish. He had seen that first-hand. 'What is it?'

She stood, walking around the table, placing a hand on his shoulder. 'Haven't you noticed, Thirio? Is that really possible?'

He frowned. Always detail orientated, he struggled to think what he might have missed.

Lucinda chuckled. 'Look.' She took his hand in hers and pressed it to her flat stomach. He stared at it, her meaning obvious, even when it didn't compute.

'Lucinda.' He jerked up to standing, his heart pounding into his throat. 'You can't be serious.'

'Oh, I am.' He grinned.

'But...you haven't been at all sick.'

'I know. I've felt wonderful.'

'But Evie—'

'Every pregnancy is different.'

'How long have you known?'

'Only a couple of weeks,' she said with an apologetic smile. 'And then I decided to wait until I was twelve weeks, just to be absolutely sure.' Her kindness was so typical of Lucinda—to try to spare him from the pain of a possible loss. 'But I had another scan yesterday.'

'Your mystery appointment!' he accused with a grin. 'I did notice you were being quite vague about your schedule.'

'I just desperately wanted to know for sure before I told you. Everything's fine. In six months we will have a lovely baby…do you want to know?'

'Not that it matters, but yes, I want to know.'

He waited, and Lucinda stepped up onto her tiptoes, whispering the gender into his ear. He pulled apart, grinning down at his wife, feeling as though the world had blessed him with a goodness he didn't deserve. Except Lucinda told him every day that he did, and Thirio was just starting to believe it.

'I hope she has your goodness, my darling wife.'

'And your heart.'

A year later, they held their six-month-old daughter in their arms, little Connie, named for his mother, as they eyed the memorial garden that had been created in the grounds of the *castile*, for his parents. Evie and Erik stood a little to the side, the twins weaving between their feet, Evie's hand pressed to her rounded stomach. Erik held her close as tears fell down Evie's cheeks. It was a poignant moment, but a necessary one. At last Constantina and Andreas Skartos's memories were brought into the light, where the good times could be remembered with joy, the gifts they'd given their children honoured daily. Grief was still a part of Thirio's heart, but it was a grief he was determined to learn from.

Life was short. Unpredictable and precious, and he was determined to make every moment of his count, just as he intended his children would.

He kissed his wife's forehead and he smiled.

He was exactly where he was meant to be, with Lucinda by his side, and life was truly, wonderfully good.

* * * * *

Swept up in the drama of
Cinderella in the Billionaire's Castle?

Then why not fall into the whirlwind of these other Clare Connelly stories?

Cinderella's Night in Venice
My Forbidden Royal Fling
Crowned for His Desert Twins
Vows on the Virgin's Terms
Forbidden Nights in Barcelona

Available now!